W9-CBS-715

HELL CREEK CABIN

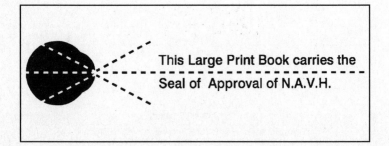

This Large Print Book carries the
Seal of Approval of N.A.V.H.

HELL CREEK CABIN

FRANK RODERUS

THORNDIKE PRESS
A part of Gale, Cengage Learning

GALE
CENGAGE Learning·

Farmington Hills, Mich • San Francisco • New York • Waterville, Maine
Meriden, Conn • Mason, Ohio • Chicago

GALE
CENGAGE Learning®

LIBRARY OF CONGRESS CATALOGING-IN-PUBLICATION DATA

Roderus, Frank.
  Hell Creek cabin / by Frank Roderus. — Large print edition.
    pages ; cm. — (Thorndike Press large print western)
    ISBN 978-1-4104-6788-1 (hardcover) — ISBN 1-4104-6788-0 (hardcover)
    1. Large type books. I. Title.
  PS3568.O346H45 2014
  813'.54—dc23   2014003222

Published in 2014 by arrangement with Hartline Literary Agency.

Printed in the United States of America
1 2 3 4 5 6 7 18 17 16 15 14

For Stephen and Mandi

CHAPTER 1

Veach ducked low along the neck of the horse in a futile effort to avoid the whippy spruce branches. They not only stung when they dragged across exposed flesh, they added insult in the form of sticky remnants of resin where they touched. It was a small thing each time. One or two or a dozen such would scarcely have been noticed. But the cumulative effect was annoying.

For perhaps the fiftieth time that afternoon he regretted having left the clear, well-marked, comfortable road leading south toward Bridger. The gentle slope leading upward and westward had looked so deceptively deep. It had beckoned with a clear invitation to avoid a half dozen days of travel or more by cutting through to the Idaho side then and there. That slope was two days behind him now, and the promise of an easy pass had proven false. Simple stubbornness was now the primary reason for him to continue forward. He told himself that he should accept the loss of time and turn back now, before he went any deeper on dead-end hope that he might find a way through. He told himself that, but he continued to ride forward. If he lost any more time the promised job might not be open when he did arrive. At this point it was a gamble whichever route he chose.

The dark spruce thinned somewhat as the underweight roan topped out on this slope and started down a slightly falling grade. If they were lucky there would be water some-where ahead and — more important — grass. There was too little forage here, far less than he had expected, and the horse was already beginning to show the lack. It had had no excess weight to start with and could ill afford a period of hard work and short feed now.

Veach sat upright again and turned the collar of his coat closer around his neck. The thick branches kept knocking the collar down no matter how often he turned it up, and the air at this altitude had an unpleas-ant bite in it. He did not know if that should be considered normal in late September, but he had not anticipated such cold. His coat and gloves were unlined and not very heavy.

He tugged his hat lower and hunched his shoulders. It did not make the cold any less, but somehow he felt better for having done it. He continued down the slope like that, a lean man just under six feet in height, thirty or a little over, a shaggy moustache extending well below the corners of his mouth. He had a beard stubble that had been accumulating for several days. He wore high-heeled boots with pointed toes like those favored by Texas cattle drovers, but his clothes had not been subjected to rough range use. His clothing was durable, but neat and well fitted.

The scattered spruce gave way abruptly to a steeper, rock-faced drop to a narrow floor several hundred feet below. A silver sheen and flicker of moving water ran through the center of the gorge. There was grass, too, in good quantity. The only problem was in getting to it. The drop here was too steep and the rock too slick for a horse to descend without mishap.

Veach turned in the saddle, trying to spot a way down. To his left the slope seemed worse, if anything. To the right the cut curved out of sight toward the northwest. The only other choice would be to retreat. He reined the horse to the right and let it pick its way deeper into the mountains at its own deliberate pace. At least Idaho was in that general direction.

The horse picked its way carefully across a weather-silvered tangle of fallen limbs and deteriorating tree trunks. The sparse, flinty soil underfoot was padded with a layer of brown, rotting needles.

He rounded the northward curve of the gorge and followed the rocky lip west for several slow miles without finding a way down. Frustratingly, below him the flat within the gorge widened; from above it looked like the grass was even higher and better here than it was downstream.

The deep cut to his left narrowed ahead. It pinched down to barely more than the width of the stream, with slick, vertical walls of hard rock on either side. At its narrowest the cut could not have been more than thirty feet across. There Veach dismounted to lead the horse across broken sheets of gray-black rock. He did not trust the animal's worn shoes on such a surface, and had no desire to chance a slip and perhaps a fall here.

Above that funnel the gorge became wider again, the bottom flat and broad, but with less grass and more rock visible than he had seen downstream. The walls here were no less steep than those behind him.

He continued to lead the tired horse, but now with a goal in mind. About a quarter of a mile ahead he could see smoke rising from the rocky floor. A tumble of house-sized rock slabs against the far wall hid the source of the smoke from his view.

Veach led the horse to a point opposite the tumbled rocks, but moved it back away from the rim before he dropped the reins to ground-tie the animal. It seemed a safe bet the horse was not going anywhere. There was certainly no forage to tempt it away, and it was too fatigued to bolt. It dropped its head and stood with all four legs spraddled wide when he let go of the reins.

He went to the edge of the rim and hunkered there to roll a cigarette while he watched the floor below him.

The thin column of pale smoke came from a small, rock-walled cabin perhaps sixteen feet square. A pole roof had been laid, although he could not see where young trees might have been cut. There were no trees at all within this part of the gorge. The poles were capped with mud. The smoke issued from a mud-and-stick chimney plastered haphazardly at the upstream end of the cabin.

Near the cabin and upstream from it was a three-sided shelter that, like the cabin, incorporated the slope itself as a back wall. The front of the shelter was partially enclosed by loosely piled rock, laid in place but not mortared or even mud-chinked. The space between the two structures was taken up by a tangle of uncut deadwood, presumably stored there against future need.

Between the cabin and the swift-running stream was a flat that showed the bedraggled remains of someone's garden. Even from a distance Veach could see that the garden had been a poorly tended scratch-and-wait affair. It was scarcely possible to differentiate between the tilled area and the native soil around it. Two winding rows of brown and withered cornstalks were the only tangible evidence of the garden's existence. From the size of the stalks he judged that they would not have been very productive.

Veach finished his cigarette, exhaling heavily after the last puff. He ground out the embers on the bare rock by his feet and let the remaining wisp of twisted paper and tobacco fall apart. A flow of air carrying the smell of distant snow and ice scattered the shreds and sent them skittering over the edge.

He stood and shifted forward as far as he dared here. Where there were people there should be access to them. He found it only a few yards up the gorge from where he stood: a steep trail and apparently an old one, probably a game trail. It was sufficiently wide to accommodate a saddle horse or a pack animal. At the lower reaches, broken, lighter rock gave indication that someone had improved on what nature and wildlife had created. It was still quite steep.

Veach went back to the roan and took up the reins. He paused to examine the animal skeptically for a moment, shook his head and led the horse to the beginning of the narrow trail. He did not mount there. Instead he slipped the bridle from the roan's head, stepped toward its rump and urged it down.

The horse laid its ears flat and balked. Veach gave it an insistent cut with the rein ends. The horse tucked its tail in tight, but it started down the path, taking short, choppy steps on braced legs. Veach was glad he had chosen to walk, for once the animal was started it could not turn back. If it stumbled or panicked he would rather watch it than ride it down.

The roan made it down safely, taking the last ten or fifteen yards in a succession of scrambling leaps. It stopped at the first meager patch of tan, brittle grass it came to and began busily cropping the stems. It made moist, snuffling sounds in its haste to eat.

Veach came down more slowly. He left the horse where it was and walked across the long, narrow flat, the bridle draped on his shoulder. He was able to leap the fast-falling stream without getting his boots wet. A few feet downstream from where he crossed was an unnaturally straight line of large rocks in the now mostly dry stream bed. No doubt at other times of the year those would serve as stepping-stones. And no doubt they would have to be replaced each spring. It was a wonder that even the cabin could be secure during the spring melt. He passed the remains of the garden. From ground level it was even more difficult to see where the rows had been scratched into the stony soil for planting.

Near the house he stopped. He pulled off one glove and tilted his hat back.

"Hello, the house," he called. "Anyone home here?"

There was no immediate response, but he thought he heard a faint noise from inside the stone cabin.

"Hello?"

The crudely built wooden door opened a crack. "Just a minute." It was a woman's voice.

For a moment Veach stood, wondering if he should collect his roan and lead it down through the funnel to the better grass below. A hot meal and someone to talk to would be welcome, but not if he were frightening the woman who lived here. Her man was obviously away from the cabin or he would have stepped outside by now. Veach was on the verge of turning away when the door opened.

The woman stepped out. "Come in." A delighted smile reinforced the spoken invitation.

Her appearance was totally unexpected in such a place — so much so that for an embarrassingly long moment Veach stared at her, unable to respond.

She was young — in her very early twenties, if that old. Pale, pale blond hair. Slender, but with an intriguingly full figure both above and below a handspan waist. Her eyes were large and very dark. They dominated delicate facial features that would not have been out of place on an exquisitely crafted cameo or the most intricately drawn miniature. Her hair was neatly curled and pinned.

Far more surprising than the person, though, was her dress. Here, days of hard travel from any town or habitation Veach had ever heard of, she was wearing no simple housedress, but a bustled, lace-fronted dress of some expensive-looking royal-blue material. It was the sort of dress one young lady might wear to call upon another for a tea-sipping afternoon of conversation.

Veach did not know what might transpire at such events, but that was what came to mind when he saw the woman. He was barely able to restrain himself from shaking his head to assure himself that his imagination had not run wild with him.

"Yes, ma'am," he said hurriedly. "Thank you." He hoped she had not noticed the lapse of time between invitation and response. It could not have been long. But there was a subtle glint of amusement in those dark eyes as she graciously stepped aside with a swish of long skirts and beckoned him through the door.

Veach removed his hat and paused to stamp his boots outside the doorway before he entered. The action was a mannerism born from what might have been expected of a caller under other circumstances and in other places. It could have no practical effect here, for the floor of the cabin was the same flinty dirt as the ground outside. There was not even a flat stone laid as a threshold to separate exterior earth from interior earthen floor.

He stopped just inside the door and took a step to the side. She followed and closed out the flow of frigid air that had been spilling into the cabin.

Unlike its occupant, the cabin was what he might have expected. A sheet metal stove to the right, with its pipe angled into the wall. A small, roughly made table dominating the center of the one tiny room. A single rope-sprung bed pegged and pounded into the far corner on the left, barely wide enough for two persons to lie side by side — at this time of day a lumpy tangle of blankets and grass-stuffed mattress. Shelves and pegs lined the walls. In the near corner to the left were piled several small trunks. The uppermost of these was unlatched, a stray corner of plain gray woolen material escaping from under the lid.

There was a nearly empty water bucket beside the stove and a few pots and utensils on a wide shelf above it. The table held a tumbled pile of hair-curling irons, a box of pins and an assortment of combs and brushes with matching backs of polished shell. A hand mirror and another on a wire stand were placed before one of the two chairs.

The cabin was dimly lighted by a single lamp suspended over the table. There were no windows to admit sunlight, and an open door would have brought in more cold than light.

"May I take your hat and coat, Mr. . . . ?"

"Oh! Yes, ma'am." He smiled awkwardly. He had not even met the woman, actually, and she already had caught him staring. Twice. He gave her the hat and started to unbutton his coat.

She waited for him to finish, calm and poised, a lady doing what was expected of her to make a visitor welcome and comfortable. Only that faint, flickering glint deep in her eyes showed any awareness of the impression she was making.

"The name is Veach, ma'am. Daniel Francis Veach, late of Bremer County, Iowa." Now why would he have answered in such a manner, he asked himself after he had heard his own voice speak the words. He had not spoken to anyone in such a pompous, silly way since high school commencement. He gave her his coat.

"It is our pleasure, Mr. Veach," she said. "I am Mrs. John Waring. My husband will join us soon. In the meantime, please make yourself comfortable." She gestured toward the crude table, her formality unhampered

18

by the coat and bridle and hat she held.

"Yes, ma'am," Veach said. He pulled out the chair opposite the mirrors and other female paraphernalia. He sat, started to cross his legs, thought better of it.

The woman hung his hat and gear on pegs near the door. She crossed to the table and unhurriedly collected her combs and curling irons. She packed them carefully into a traveling case made of fine-grained, polished leather. "I'll have coffee on in a moment, Mr. Veach."

She bent to pick up the water bucket and started toward the door. Veach jumped to his feet and reached for the rope bail of the bucket.

"I'd be glad to do that for you, ma'am," he said. "And would it be all right if I pull the saddle off my horse for a little while?"

"Of course. I should have thought to mention it."

He took his hat and bridle from the peg, but did not bother with the coat. That was a mistake, he decided as soon as he was outside. Either it was growing colder or he had not realized how cold he had been before he felt the cozy stove-warmth of the thick-walled cabin.

The roan had moved closer while he was inside. It was grazing on the slightly better

19

grass nearer the stream. He left the bucket beside the creek and crossed to the horse.

Veach flipped the reins around the neck of the animal and held them loosely at the throat. He led the horse to Waring's shed, hobbled it and pulled his saddle. He turned the horse loose and dropped his saddle to the ground outside the unfinished front wall of the shed. The interior of the shed held a thick accumulation of manure. Wherever Waring was, he had his animals with him.

Veach dropped the bridle onto his saddle and thought for a moment, wondering what among his provisions he could spare. He decided on a packet of tea — it seemed appropriate here — and dug it out of the nearly depleted sack tied behind his bedroll.

He was shivering and runny-nosed by the time he retrieved and filled the bucket and returned to the cabin.

"Here's your water, ma'am. And some tea if you can use it."

"That is very thoughtful of you, Mr. Veach," she said. She smiled prettily as she accepted the heavy bucket and the paper-wrapped twist of dried leaves. "I have coffee freshly ground, or would you prefer the tea now?"

"The coffee would be fine, ma'am."

She was dimpled and pretty and gay, but

he wished Waring would hurry home. Veach was not altogether comfortable with a woman who could be so fancily formal out here in the mountains.

CHAPTER 2

It was nearly dark before Waring returned home. The woman had already started preparing the evening meal, insisting that Veach spend the night. Her husband, she said, would be disappointed if he did not stay. They had visitors so seldom. And John could tell him about conditions deeper in the mountains, might know of some trails that would help him on his way. That argument was more telling than the dictates of politeness.

Throughout the afternoon she had sat at the table with him, sipping coffee and grilling him for the last and smallest detail she could pry from his memory about the current fashions he had seen on the streets of Bozeman. He was sure he was a disappointment to her — it was not the sort of thing at which he was expert — but he did his best to remember and was himself surprised at some of the things her prodding brought to mind.

Still, he was relieved when he heard the approach of hooves.

"It must be your husband, ma'am. I'll go see if I can help him with anything."

"Tell him supper will be ready in a few minutes," she said brightly.

"Yes, ma'am," he agreed, but he did not see how that could be. She had not done much more so far than begin to mix a dough concoction of some sort and put a pan of water on to heat.

Veach got his hat and coat and pulled on his gloves before he opened the door and slipped quickly out into the early twilight, not much brighter now than the dark interior of the cabin.

Waring was by the shed, unloading canvas sacks from a trio of fat mules. He was a small man, perhaps five feet seven, and quite slender, but Veach received no impression of weakness in him. For some reason Waring made him think of a rawhide *reata,* thin but tremendously durable and resilient. The man had sandy-colored hair and was clean-shaven. His expression was mild, almost diffident, but his pale gray eyes were cool and probing. His face was flushed, possibly from recent exertion in the still deepening cold.

Veach introduced himself. "Give you a

hand with those?" he offered.

"I can manage. Thanks," Waring said. He turned back to his chore, piling the sacks against the half-finished front wall of the shed. "I'm sure Ann was delighted to see you come by," he said over his shoulder as he worked. "We don't get many visitors out here." Waring did not sound as if he shared his wife's delight. He was polite, but certainly not delighted.

He unstrapped the pack saddles and piled them beside the sacks. As soon as the mules had had a chance to roll he led them into the shed. "You're welcome to put your horse in here for the night," he offered. "I lost two good mules to a cat or a bear, whatever it is that's prowling the rocks around here."

"Guess I'd better do it then," Veach said. He thought it curious that a man would choose to make his home in such an out-of-the-way place and yet not be able to identify the predator taking his livestock, but he offered no comment on the oddity. He took his horse by the forelock and led it into the low shed. The three mules shifted their rumps toward the newcomer and stamped nervously at the dirt floor in the far end of the narrow shed.

Waring retrieved two peeled poles from the floor inside the door opening and wedged them in place at chest and waist levels as a barrier.

"We might have some squealing and kicking," the man said, "but they should be safe enough except from each other. I haven't seen anything close to the house."

Veach mumbled his agreement. The horse and mules should be able to get along together once they worked out a pecking order. If there were no tracks close it was likely a cat doing the raiding. Bears tend to lose their fear of man-smell if they are unmolested and could be expected to prowl close if a source of food was penned away from them.

Veach was mildly curious about the sacks Waring had hauled in from his labors, but the man gave every impression of having forgotten their existence once they were dumped onto the ground. He did not even glance toward them again.

Waring slapped his hands together. His gloves were ragged and badly worn. "Let's go in by the fire and see if there is some food available. A hot meal will taste awfully good tonight, I'll tell you."

"It should be ready," Veach said. "Your missus was fixing it before I came out."

"Good." Waring smiled and motioned the taller man ahead of him.

They went into the cabin, opening the door barely wide enough to allow a swift entry. The sudden warmth inside was almost overpowering. Veach could imagine how good it must feel to Waring if he had been working outdoors all day. After just those few minutes of it Veach's cheeks tingled faintly from the warmth of the collapsible stove.

Ann Waring smiled cheerfully at her husband and their guest when the two men entered. She left the stove, ignoring a pan of water that was threatening to boil over, and came to help Waring out of his bulky coat, taking the garment from him and turning to hang it on a peg before she planted a brief kiss on his cheek and returned to the stove. A bubbling hiss of steam announced that her return had been a fraction of a minute too slow.

Veach wondered idly what her greeting would have been had there not been a guest present. Then, realizing with wry awareness the impropriety of such a thought, he shoved the question aside. Even if he did know the answer it would have been no business of his.

She snatched the pan from the stove and placed it to the side of the firebox surface where the metal would not be quite so hot.

"Take a seat, gentlemen," she said happily. "Everything seems to be ready, and all at the same time." To Veach she said, "I'm really quite a frightful cook. John is a dear to be so patient with me." Despite the meaning of the words her tone clearly said that she did not herself consider cooking to be an accomplishment of any great note or importance.

"Nonsense, dear. You do very well," Waring assured her.

She gave him a pleased smile. Her eyes widened after a moment, and she said, "Why, John . . . Where on earth have you put today's ore? Won't you be smelting to-ni . . . ?" She chopped the words off abruptly when she saw the quick glare of warning and anger he shot at her. "Oh," she exclaimed contritely. She looked from one man to the other, her eyes finally coming to a stop again on her husband. "I'm sorry."

Waring avoided looking at her. To Veach he said, "Sit down, please. Our supper will be cold if we don't begin soon." There was a false ring of forced heartiness in his tone.

The woman stopped in the act of transferring boiled meat into a bowl. "John, what did I . . . ? I mean . . . ?"

Waring still did not look at her. He took one of the two chairs at the table and examined his empty plate.

"Ma'am," Veach said tentatively, "your husband is absolutely right. You folks don't know me from Adam's off ox. Why, I could be any kind of a thief. Or worse. It's best not to say too much among strangers."

"I see." She finished what she had been doing and set the meat on the table. She added a bowl of undercooked corn cakes and retired to perch on the edge of the bunk. She took up a needle and darning egg and an untidy heap of tattered socks. She must have had three pairs of unmended socks in her lap, Veach noticed. They had been piling up for some time.

Waring gave him a covert look of gratitude and gestured toward the bowls. "Help yourself, Mr. Veach."

"You bet."

The woman had been right. She was quite a frightful cook. And a pan of boiling water was not his idea of the way to cook meat to start with. Still, it was hot food, and the woman seemed to be doing her best to make him feel welcome.

When they were done eating Veach leaned back with an exaggerated sigh of contentment to show his thanks. He built a cigarette and offered his pouch of flaked tobacco to Waring.

The other man hesitated a moment before he accepted the pouch. "If you don't mind then . . . It has been awhile since I had any tobacco." He left the table to rummage in a dark corner of the cabin. When he returned he had a pipe, a chunk of smoothed and shaped brierroot with an oversized bowl shaped much like a coal scuttle. The charred and blackened bowl had a look of long and honorable service. Waring took a pinch of the loose tobacco and reached deep into the pipe to pack it.

"Hell, man, that's not enough to get that old thing warm," Veach protested. "Pack it full. I've got plenty to last me over into Idaho, so don't be shy."

Waring nodded gratefully and filled the massive bowl. He found a match near the stove and made a production of allowing the sulfur to burn away before he carefully started embers glowing across the entire top surface of the tobacco. When he was done he sat back and nodded again. "Now that is fine, Veach. Damned fine. I had nearly forgotten how much I enjoy my after-dinner smoke."

"The flake cut isn't much in a pipe, but better than nothing, I guess."

Waring smiled. "Much better."

Veach was aware of Ann Waring busying

29

herself in the shadows. She cleared the dishes and began washing them. She had not eaten anything. When she was finished with the few dishes she poured hot water into a crockery teapot and carefully tapped in a small portion of the tea leaves Veach had brought.

The mere idea of serving tea to a visitor seemed to vitalize her. Her eyes danced and sparkled, and soon her husband warmed under the spell of good feeling she cast into the smallest crack and crevice of the tiny cabin. The tea even seemed to chase the wispy, unseen tendrils of chill that had been creeping through the mortared stone walls during the meal.

Waring stood when they were done and stretched expansively. "Jove, but I feel fit now. It is the way a man *should* feel when his day's work is done." He opened the stove door and filled the box with fresh lengths of split wood.

When he turned back toward the table Waring cocked his head and looked at his guest for a long moment. At length he seemed to shrug, although his shoulders did not actually move. The gesture was more implied than made.

"Ann has already let the cat out of the bag, Mr. Veach. I may as well go ahead with my work so I don't get too far behind. Would you mind?"

"Of course not. Can I help?"

"You could help me bring the ore inside if it wouldn't be too much bother."

They bundled back into their coats and gloves. When Waring opened the door the sudden cold was bitterly shocking. Involuntarily both men hesitated in the open doorway as if the act of stepping through the opening would plunge them into icy water rather than the cold night air. The temperature seemed to be continuing the dizzy plummet it had begun that afternoon.

Hunched and tight-muscled against the cold, they hurried to the livestock shed. Waring grabbed the topmost of the bags he had piled there earlier. It took them three trips to complete the transfer into the cabin. Before they were done, in those few moments, Veach's fingertips were in pain from the cold.

On their last trip back to the cabin Waring paused and tilted his head to look at the night sky between the rock walls towering above them. "Clouds," he said.

"The cold won't get any worse then," Veach suggested.

Waring shivered. "That is what I'm afraid of. Cold can be fought. But if we were to get a heavy snow now . . ." He shook his head. "I wasn't expecting this so soon. I hoped to be out first. Just a few more weeks . . ." His voice tailed away.

"You shouldn't have anything to worry about this early," Veach said. "In a couple more months, sure. Even next month. But it's still September, man. Barely the fall of the year."

Waring gave him a small, wry smile. "You don't know these mountains well, do you?"

Veach shook his head, and Waring sighed.

"I couldn't claim to know them either," Waring said, "but I listen very well indeed when knowledgeable men speak. And I know enough to be afraid."

"Then we'll both hope you're wrong."

"I think that would be a very good idea."

They went inside to the welcome heat of the cabin. The sudden warmth sent prickly tingles of feeling through numbed fingers and icy earlobes, and their noses began to drip in a most undignified manner. Ann Waring did not appear to notice their furtive sleeve-swipes under their noses.

"Is there anything I can do, dear?" she asked.

"No. Thanks."

She smiled at him and bent over her darning. Veach thought she was taking an ex-

32

traordinary amount of time with the task.

The ore Waring had collected was pale quartz, scantily ribboned with bright threads of gold. Veach offered to pulverize the brittle rock while Waring melted and collected the gold. Even with both of them working at the chore it took several hours to complete. When they were done Waring had a cooling, round-topped disk of yellow metal that Veach thought might be worth seventy-five or eighty dollars. It was a handsome return for a day's work.

"If you'll tell me where to dump it, I'll carry this trash out for you," Veach offered.

"Here, I'll show you. There's more than one load."

They dumped the dross against the gorge wall at the downstream end of the cabin. There was already a large drift of pulverized and discarded rock there. Neither man commented on the temperature. It seemed to be rising.

Veach took a last load out by himself. When he returned the lump of nearly pure gold was no longer in sight, nor had he expected it to be. Veach closed the door firmly behind him, removed his coat and shook melting droplets of water from his hat.

"Snow," he said.

Ann Waring paid no special attention to the single word Veach dropped flatly into the close air of the cabin, but her husband gave Veach a long, unreadable look. Veach knew the man was worried. Perhaps he had a right to be.

CHAPTER 3

Now that her husband's work was safely out of the way and her own slip in mentioning it might be forgotten, Ann Waring displayed a poorly contained eagerness to return to tea and conversation. Veach got the impression that she could have spent the remainder of the night that way happily, but Waring rebuffed her none-too-subtle suggestions. The man had a right to be tired if he was working a hard-rock dig single-handed, Veach thought.

"It's time we got to bed," Waring said. "I have work to do tomorrow, and I'm sure Mr. Veach will want an early start."

Waring sounded worried. No doubt a man with a gold pocket and a good-looking woman would want passing strangers to continue their passing as quickly as possible. A storm could change that and perhaps could alter other things as well. The man had said he intended to be out before the first snow. If he let his woman face trouble now he was certain to blame himself. Veach decided Waring might have every reason to worry.

"Do you have bedding?" Waring asked.

"My bedroll is still out by your shed," Veach said. "I didn't think to bring it in earlier."

"If you'll give me a hand here," — Waring turned to the pile of boxes and an uncovered trunk — "we can hang blankets in front of our bed. You should be comfortable by the stove tonight, don't you think?"

"Sure. That sounds fine to me."

They tacked two end-hung blankets to the roof poles to form a screen and separate the bunk from the rest of the cabin. It made the tiny cabin seem even smaller.

"It will take me a few minutes to find everything if you, uh, need some privacy in here," Veach said.

Waring nodded gratefully. "We won't take long," he promised.

Veach bundled himself ear-deep into his thin coat before he went out. He opened the door barely wide enough to slip through. Outside he was met by stinging, wind-driven spicules of snow. The first light and puffy flakes he had seen earlier had already changed into the small, grainy particles that often ride the winds of hard storm weather.

It occurred to Veach that he had not seen an outhouse near the cabin. Surely, he thought, they did not trouble themselves with the constant nuisance of slop jars. Not that it was his affair, he reminded himself. Such things just made a man curious about the habits of other people. He hunched himself against the cold and slipped between the bars across the opening to Waring's mule shelter.

In the protection of the walls he was partially shielded from the wind and so felt at least a little warmer. He shoved his horse aside and relieved himself against the back wall. The body heat of the horse radiated into the rock-walled corner of the shed, so he remained there while he rolled and smoked a cigarette. One cigarette should give them enough time to prepare for the night, he decided. It was definitely too cold for him to want to stay for another.

He unstrapped his bedroll from his saddle and moved the saddle to the downwind side of the animal shelter — between it and the cabin — while he could still find it. Melting snow between rump and saddle was not a sensation to court if there was any way to avoid it. He dropped the saddle in the protection of the wall and quickstepped ahead of the driving force of the wind back to the cabin. At least, going with the wind, his coat collar stayed up. Snow driving in under his hat brim lanced needle sharp against the backs of his ears.

He reached the door and paused to knock. "Come," Waring called from inside.

Veach stood, red-faced and shivering, inside the door. He stamped snow from his boots and shook more off his hat and the back of his coat. Waring did not have to ask about the conditions outside.

Ann Waring was out of sight behind the blanket screen. Veach could hear a faint creak of rope and the low rustle of the grass mattress as she shifted on the bed.

"Do you need anything, Mr. Veach?" Waring offered.

Veach was struck anew by the man's formality and that of his wife. Outside the cities, particularly the railroad towns where access was easy, a man could go for months in this country without hearing the word "mister." Both Warings used it frequently. "Nothing, thanks. I'll spread my things here and be just fine."

Waring nodded. He removed his boots and trousers and shirt, folded the clothing carefully and laid it out of sight behind the curtain. "Good night then." He stepped between the blankets, and Veach could hear the twanging pull of taut rope.

Veach untied his bedroll and spread it between the stove and the table before he blew out the lamp. There was barely enough floor room to accommodate the bedding.

He did not know if Waring wanted him to maintain the fire overnight and somehow, now that the Warings were in bed, he did not want to ask. That was irrational, he knew. They could not yet have had time to fall asleep, and his voice would carry through the blankets as if they were not there. Still, he decided against it. Had the man wanted him to do so he could have asked.

Veach pulled off his boots and belt, but left his clothes on. He lay on his bedding; it was neither softer nor harder here than it would have been outside, but he was infinitely warmer and more comfortable beside this sheltered stove than he would have been out in the driving wind and snow. He stared for a time at the winking red eye of the stove draft and slipped eventually into shallow sleep.

Both men were awake early the next morning. Veach sat up first and pulled the blankets of his bedroll close around his shoulders. A deep, brittle chill seeped through the rock walls of the cabin and lay ominously in the air. As quietly as he could Veach lifted the latch of the firebox door on the stove beside him. He used a billet of fat wood to stir into the mostly cold ashes of last night's fire and when he found a small bed of still-glowing coals he reconstructed the blaze, one careful stick after another. He could feel the effects almost immediately. It would take longer for the warmth to reach into the blanketed alcove shared by the Warings.

The stove door hinges protested only faintly when he pressed the closure shut, but almost immediately after Waring stuck his head between the suspended blankets. His head disappeared and Veach heard the ropes creak as Waring shifted position on the bed. The man's feet shoved into view and the rest of him followed. He stood in the small, cold room shivering and rubbing sleep from his eyes. His hair was tousled, and his woolen underwear hung limp and baggy at the knees and buttocks.

"Hope I didn't wake you," Veach said softly. "I thought you'd want the place warm before your missus gets up."

Waring nodded and tried unsuccessfully to stifle a yawn. " 'S all right. Time to get up anyway." He rubbed his rump and shook himself, then stepped into his trousers and pulled his boots on. He seemed more awake then. He sat in one of the chairs. After a moment Veach saw that Waring's head was cocked slightly to one side and he seemed to be listening intently to something outside.

Veach could not understand at first what had caught Waring's attention. Try as he might, Veach could hear no sound at all from beyond the walls.

"The wind," he whispered with sudden comprehension. "The storm let up."

"I hope so," Waring said cautiously. He stood and walked to the door. There he paused for a moment with a work-hardened hand on the iron latch before he tilted it free and pulled the door a few inches inward.

There was no need for him to comment. Veach could see in the man's face the scene Waring was witnessing outside the door. He could see it there even more clearly than in the tumble of packed white flakes that fell through that narrow gap onto the cabin floor at the base of the door.

"Still falling?" Veach asked.

Waring pushed the door closed. When he turned toward Veach he looked sick. He nodded. In his expression was the agony of self-condemnation.

"It can't be that bad," Veach said. He came to his feet and walked sock-footed to the door. He pulled the door ajar and looked out.

At the bottom of the cabin door the snow was not more than eight inches deep. Hillocks and wind-rippled waves of snow were spread across the floor of the deep gorge. Higher drifts were built like conical buttresses against the far rock wall. Dense, heavy flakes continued to fall from a steel-gray sky. Except for the drifts, Veach thought, the snow cover would not be much more than a foot deep anywhere that he could see.

"Aw, that's no problem," Veach said. "A horse or mule wouldn't even notice anything that light." He felt relieved. From Waring's reaction he had been genuinely fearful of what he might see.

Veach smiled. "But for a fact it doesn't look now like I'll be crossing deeper into this range before spring. Look, if you want to go out now, we can go together. That would give us four animals to change off breaking trail, and two men in case there is trouble. Between us we'll get along just fine. Of course," he added, "if you want to stay, that's up to you. I was just assuming you want to go out, the way you were talking last night."

Waring shook his head in annoyance. He pulled the door out of Veach's hand and yanked it wide, destroying the gains made so far by the new fire in the stove.

"Look again," he said. He seemed to be unaware of the cold. "There is a crust under that new snow. Sometime last night, say after the wind died and before the new fall started, the temperature rose enough to glaze the surface. Look across at those drifts. The first fall was wind-driven." He shoved the door closed. "Can't you see what that means?"

"Now that you ask, no sir, I guess I don't if you think there is some big problem. What I see is a snowfall we can get through just fine."

Both men had forgotten their intention to be quiet for Ann Waring's benefit. Their voices, even at a normal level, filled the tiny cabin and reverberated from the surrounding stone walls.

Waring's realized fears became quick anger directed at Veach's lack of understanding. "Below us, to the east, there is a narrow gap. The wind won't have been able to drive through there. It will have eddied like so much water against rock, dropping the snow it was carrying. That gap will be closed

43

now. It will certainly be impassable for a horse or a mule. A man *might* cross over the drifts. A horse never could." He stabbed a finger toward the far wall beyond the closed and silent doorway. "There is a path up that face, Veach. You saw the crust, didn't you? That pathway will be impossible to climb now. A saddle or pack animal could never climb it with a glaze on the rock. I doubt that you or I could. *Now* do you understand?"

"What about the other direction?" Veach asked patiently.

Waring grunted. "There is a rock ladder on this side near my dig. We might be able to get up, but it would be pointless without horses. Beyond that it would be . . . I would say another seventeen miles to the next remotely possible way out for a mule. And that is not a good path either — only slightly easier than the ascent on the other wall here. I am afraid," — he shrugged — "we may be here for some time."

"Surely you must be wrong, Waring. There is so little snow out there now and . . ."

"Dammit, Veach, I am not," Waring snapped impatiently. "We are stuck here until a chinook opens one of those routes out."

A heavy rustling of the mattress from

44

behind the screen, only feet away in the close quarters, told them Ann Waring was awake and getting dressed. Waring looked bleak when he realized his wife would already have heard about their situation. He had intended to break the news to her more gently than through his unreasoned anger with Veach.

Veach understood. He gave Waring a sympathetic look and filled the silence by saying, "Look, we don't know yet that you're right. You can't see that narrow spot from here. Why don't you and I go down and take a look. It might not be closed at all. Then we'd all have been worrying for nothing."

Waring nodded gratefully. "You're right, of course." He raised his voice slightly. "Ann, Mr. Veach and I are going out for a while. Will you have breakfast ready in an hour, please?"

"Of course, dear. And bring some wood in when you come, would you?" The blankets bulged as she moved against them on the other side.

Veach had a sudden and unwelcome vision of her removing her nightshift so she could dress. His face flushed hotly and he wished a desperate hope that he would not be confined in this too-small cabin for long.

Waring appeared not to have noticed his blush and could not in any event know the cause of it. Still Veach was uncomfortable.

The men bundled into their coats and gloves, and Waring wrapped a woolen shawl around his ears in preference to wearing a hat. Veach took his bridle from the wall peg and wrapped his fist around the curved mouthpiece of the bit so that it would not chill before he put it into the horse's mouth.

"Ready?"

"Uh-huh."

They stepped out into the cold, not so extreme now as it had been the evening before, but shocking just the same after the relative warmth of the cabin. Snow continued to fall lightly. Under other circumstances it would have been a picture-pretty snowfall. Under the smoothly sculptured layer of snow the gorge did not look so bleak and barren. The towering rock faces on both sides were highlighted by clinging snow and ice. The only vegetation visible from where they stood was a straggling line of yellow-brown cornstalk tops at the crest of one of the snow waves. The creek ran like a cold, black line drawn against the white floor — a giant child's wavering, weaving line drawn with charcoal on a massive sheet of paper.

Waring scuffed his boot in the layer of

light snow accumulating on the ground. He gave Veach a look that might have been triumphant had its significance put less worry into his expression. Beneath the new snow was a hard, slick crust that faintly crunched underfoot, beneath the muffling weight of the more recently fallen snow.

"We still need to see that gap," Veach said.

They walked to the three-sided mule shelter. Some snow had driven in through the partially open front of the shed, to be trampled into an ugly brown custard under milling hooves, but the animals were well haired and were warm out of reach of the wind. Condensation rimed their whiskers and their breath blew out in white jets from their nostrils, but they seemed not to notice the weather. If anything, it would be less annoying to them than the flies of warmer seasons.

"Better feed them later, don't you think?" Veach asked.

"I have no feed," Waring said. "I've been allowing them to graze below the, uh, hole where I work." He caught the look Veach gave him. "I didn't intend to be here for the first snow, after all. Until now I thought the grass would be all I would need."

Veach nodded without speaking. It was a reasonable enough explanation, especially

47

since it would have been difficult to haul grain in and time-consuming to cut the sparse wild grasses for hay. Veach tried to remind himself that he would have done the same thing had he been in Waring's position. Still, Veach was left with a flavor of mild annoyance at Waring's lack of preparation.

"I suppose I should turn them out anyway," Waring said. "They can paw their way to the grass fairly well."

"It's better than nothing," Veach agreed. He bridled and saddled his roan while Waring hobbled his mules and turned them out. They headed immediately for what was left of the cornstalks and began breaking down the snow ridge there.

"You're turning them all loose?"

"I prefer to walk. Really," Waring said.

Veach shrugged. "Suit yourself." Like most men who had spent much time in this country of few people and distant horizons, he now rode by habit even if he had only a city block to travel. Yet as a boy he had thought nothing of a five-mile walk to visit a friend or to call on a pretty girl, and it would never have occurred to him to saddle one of the heavy draft horses they kept for farm work.

The roan was feeling better now after a

night's rest. It fidgeted as he stepped into the saddle, slipped on the uncertain footing between the shelter and the creek and nearly dumped him before he was well seated. Veach looked at Waring and said, "I guess that makes your point better than anything either of us could say."

"I'm afraid so."

If the horse had difficulty with the footing on level ground, any climb was certain to be impossible.

Waring let Veach lead the way down the gorge, the horse breaking the light snow ahead of him, although the snow depth so far could only be considered an annoyance.

They rounded the huge slabs of rock that had screened their view of the narrows below. From a quarter of a mile distant it was already clear what they would find, but Veach stubbornly pushed ahead for a closer examination, just in case the drift did not run deep into the gap. Perhaps, he was hoping, they could dig their way through if it was only ridged.

But it was not. The defile was plugged to a depth of a dozen feet or more where the wind-driven snow had been dropped out of the swirling air.

"I sure as hell hate to say you're right, Waring."

The man sighed. "No more than I wish I'd been wrong." He smiled. "Shall we go back? Ann should have our breakfast ready by now."

CHAPTER 4

"How long do you think, Waring?"

The man shrugged eloquently. "Who could say? A week. A month. Next June. No one could know."

"John!" His wife's voice was shrill with alarm. "Don't even think about us having to stay here very long. We couldn't. You *know* we couldn't."

"I know we have no choice, dear. I'm sorry. It's my fault we stayed so late, but there's no way to change it now."

"Nobody could've figured a snow this early," Veach protested. "And even if you did, why, no one could've guessed such a little bit of snow would keep anyone here. It was luck, plain and simple. Lousy luck, but luck all the same."

Ann Waring served what appeared to be their normal breakfast, although Veach thought it a strange meal for a man who spent his days doing heavy work with pick and shovel. It was a boiled corn-meal mush. It tasted like little or nothing had been added to the ground corn, and there was no sugar or tinned milk offered to improve the bland flavor.

Waring and Veach had the chairs at the table. The woman took a bowl and spoon and sat on the edge of the bed to have her breakfast. While they were out she had made the bed and tied the screening blankets back with bits of twine. The effect was almost attractive.

"I surely am sorry to be loading myself onto you folks at a time like this," Veach said, "but maybe there'll be something I can do to help. And of course I'll pitch what I've got into the pot. Lord knows it's little enough. I'd figured to stock up at Bridger and not ask my horse to carry too much at a time. But what I've got is yours to use."

"As you said, Mr. Veach, you didn't anticipate this any more than we did. No apology is necessary." He sighed. "But I am afraid we haven't much either. We really intended to be out of here several weeks ago, but . . . my lead was opening somewhat. Things seemed to be going so well. I thought we could stay just a little longer." He smiled bitterly. "I'd set myself a goal. Nearly reached it, too, and the vein widening . . . I yielded to the temptation, pushed that last little bit. Now that it's too late I have wonderful hindsight, you see. Now I'd very happily turn rabbit and run for Bridger with you if we had half a chance."

"That's the way, isn't it?" Veach said. "When you think things are going right, watch out. You're about to get hit with something."

"The fates, Mr. Veach?"

"The furies, Mr. Waring. At least that seems to be as good an answer as any other. Those old Greeks believed it. Me, I don't know. If I did I'd be a wise man — maybe a rich one, too. Instead all I am is worried."

"Please. Both of you. Stop talking like that," Ann Waring pleaded. "It will be all right in a few days. That snow will melt, and John will show us the way down to Fort Bridger, and we can take a train for home. Why, in a week we'll look on this as a lark. I know we will."

"I hope you're absolutely right, dear," Waring said. He gave her a smile of encouragement, but neither he nor Veach was willing to be so optimistic.

The men pushed their bowls and spoons aside. Veach was still hungry, but they would all be doing without seconds until they were out of the mountains.

"I'll bring the rest of my things in," Veach said. "Why don't you come with me?"

Waring nodded his comprehension. He had had opportunity to see that the remainder of Veach's possessions were contained in a single small sack that he could not possibly need help with. Both men pulled their coats on and went outdoors. The snow was continuing its light fall.

"What is it, Mr. Veach?" Waring asked as soon as they were away from the cabin.

"Look, man, you seem to know these mountains a lot better than I do, and I've heard enough stories about the hard winters up here to believe it could be quite a while — say a month — before it opens up again. And it might not do it at all. What I was thinking was this. We can't get your wife and your, uh, things, out of here with those mules. But a man on foot might make it down. How far would a man have to go to do that?"

"Um. I did think of that. But I don't know." He tipped his head back and took a long look at the solid, gray cloud cover that lay heavy and snow-laden above them. "At the very least it is more than fifty miles to the nearest dwellings that I know about. Closer to sixty, I would say. And there are a number of places below here that should be

54

drifted. A lone man trying to go out on foot could be caught in one of those drifts and never be seen again. The first melt would carry his body to God knows where. Two men would have a better chance, but . . ."

"No, I wasn't thinking of two, Waring. You couldn't leave your missus alone here. If the two didn't get through, she'd be helpless."

"I know," Waring said bleakly. He shook his head. "I really doubt that one man could do it. If the snow stops, so at least he would have easy going in the open areas, then it might, just might, be possible. If he had to fight through fifty miles of deep snow . . ."

"Yeah. Ain't that the truth."

"We'll have to wait a little longer, Mr. Veach. See what the snow does. If it stops soon perhaps I should make the attempt."

"No, I figure if one of us goes it should be me," Veach said quietly.

"It is my responsibility to . . ."

"The hell," Veach insisted. "Your job is taking care of your woman. Besides, man, from where I sit I have as big a stake in this as you. My neck is on the line here too. I'd kinda like to keep it."

Veach got his burlap sack of provisions, and Waring picked up an armload of wood to take in as an excuse for leaving the cabin. "We still have to wait and see," Waring said.

"There's no reason to argue now about which of us should try to get out."

Veach knew the quandary Waring would find himself in if one of them did try to go out on foot. Either way he would be entrusting Ann Waring's safety to a complete stranger. If Veach stayed at the cabin he would be left in isolation with the woman with no certainty that her husband would ever be seen again. Yet if Veach was the one to leave, Waring would not know whether Veach would try to return if he did reach safety. And Veach really did not know the way out from here. He would have far less chance than Waring to reach a settlement. It would be a poor choice for a man to have to make, Veach thought.

They returned to the cabin and stamped the clinging snow from their boots. The snow began to melt into muddy puddles on the bare dirt of the cabin floor.

"It is very kind of you to share with us, Mr. Veach," Ann Waring said with a dimpled smile. She seemed to be regarding their situation as a holiday, with the added pleasure of having a guest in their home. The gravity of it did not appear to affect her.

The woman unloaded Veach's food sack onto the table and exclaimed with delight at what she found there. A few pounds of rice.

A few more of dried beans. The cloth-wrapped remnants, mostly rind now, of a piece of salt pork. A double handful of ground coffee. One can of evaporated milk. A small, sticky-sweet clump of dried peaches. It was little enough. He had not expected to be so long between towns and cursed himself anew at his lack of foresight, but he did it silently and the woman did not seem to notice.

"Look, John," she said excitedly. "Fruit. And sweet, too." She gave Veach one of her sudden, brilliant smiles and said, "It has been *so* long since we've had sweets in the house. And I declare, I just *adore* sweets."

"Then you should have a piece, ma'am."

"Gentlemen?" She offered the lump of fruit. Both men declined. "Just a tiny sliver for me then," she said. With a neatly filed and buffed fingernail she peeled a narrow slice of the fruit from the lump and popped it into her mouth. Somehow she reminded Veach of a small child toying with a ball of carameled popcorn. "Um. Yum!"

Her husband smiled at her. She savored the bit of fruit for a moment and began putting Veach's things with their own supplies.

"Is there any work that needs to be done inside, Waring? I'm a fair hand at braiding horsehair or stitching leather. Kinda hate to sit around like a dummy waiting for the snow to quit if there's work that can be done."

Waring shook his head. "Not really. I already have more pack saddles and rigging than I have mules. We could get some wood cut, I suppose. I've been throwing deadwood down from above and sawing it to length as I needed it. We could cut and stack what is there. I don't believe we could go up after more for a while."

"Fine." Veach buttoned his coat and pulled his gloves back on. The activity would be a relief. He found himself vaguely uncomfortable confined inside the cabin with Waring and his wife.

They went out and set to work, the exertion keeping them comfortable except for the icy runnels of melting snow that crept underneath their coat collars. Veach used Waring's bow saw to cut the wood into stove-lengths while Waring used his ax to split them. As a precaution they started a pile of firebox-ready wood next to the cabin door where it would be easy to reach if the weather turned for the worse.

"What about the animals?" Waring asked when they took a breather. The man's face was full of color from the cold and the labor, but his breathing was steady and he showed no sign that the effort was affecting him in any way.

Veach, in contrast, was breathing heavily. Now that he was resting a film of sweat on his forehead felt like an ice-water mask, and he could feel the warm sweat beginning to chill under his arms and down his torso. The cold quickly slipped beneath his thin coat and began to make him uncomfortable.

"Leave them be," Veach said. "There's nothing else we can do for them. They'll make out on their own or they won't make out at all."

Waring nodded, but he leaned on his ax and looked worriedly across the gorge floor to where the three mules and Veach's horse were nosing in the snow under the far wall. The smooth, white perfection of the snow cover had been scarred and rumpled across a half-acre patch where the animals had been foraging. Neither man could tell how successful the animals were being in their search for food.

"We think we know so much," Waring reflected. "We believe we are so smart. We can rip metals out of the earth and bend them to our will. We build steam engines and lay rails across the entire continent to carry ourselves and our goods. We can leave a ship in New York one day and board another just like it at San Francisco in less than a week. We can send a message across thousands of miles of telegraph wire in a fraction of even that time. Yet a simple snowfall, Veach, makes us unable to do so much as care for our livestock. We could perish here, all three of us, and no one might even know it." He shook his head and picked up his ax. Absently he brushed an accumulation of snow from the tempered steel of the head.

"You're talking awful heavy, Waring. You don't know, man. We might ride out of here tomorrow. Why, I saw a chinook in Montana once. Came down from nowhere in the middle of January, and inside of twenty-four hours you'd have had to really search to find a snowbank big enough to cool a keg of beer in. Another twenty-four and you couldn't have done it no matter how hard you looked. For a week there it felt like the middle of May."

"Can we count on that to happen here?" Waring asked facetiously.

"Every bit as much as we can count on being trapped here until next June, man."

Waring gave him a smile, weak but true. "Your point is taken, Mr. Veach. In the meantime we'll do what we can and leave the remainder to the fates. Or to the furies."

"Are you a prayerful man, Waring?"

"I used to be."

"This might be a good time to take it up again. In fact, I think I'll take my own advice about that. Those furies just naturally scare hell out of me, sir."

Waring laughed, but he said, "I just might do that, too." They returned to their work, and the door-side pile of wood crept up the stone face of the cabin.

About noon Ann Waring stepped outside. She had a woolen shawl wrapped tightly around her head, and she was bundled inside a blanket like a reservation Indian. She looked small and vulnerable under the blanket.

"What should I do about dinner, John?" she asked.

Waring set his ax aside and looked at Veach, who was wiping freezing sweat from his forehead. Waring still was showing no outward signs of exertion. Waring raised his eyebrows in inquiry and got back a brief, negative shake of the head.

"Oh, I don't think so, dear. Two meals a day should be plenty." He smiled at her. "We won't be doing much physical work, you know, once this wood is cut. So I think not. You go ahead and have a bite if you wish."

She bit her lip. "I have some mush left over from breakfast. I could put that in water and make a gruel, John. It wouldn't be anything but warmth, really, but even that might be good for you. And I'm sure you could use the rest."

"All right, dear. That's very thoughtful of you. We'll be in in a few minutes, then." When she was gone Waring turned and said, "Mr. Veach, I certainly hope you can learn to enjoy cornmeal mush. Cornmeal is just about all we have left in any quantity, and there is only so much a person can do with the stuff."

Veach grinned. "Have you learned to, uh, enjoy it, Waring?"

"Well-l-l-l . . . I wouldn't go quite that far. But I'm working on it. Yes indeed, I'm working on it."

They worked a short while longer and went inside. The warmth inside the cabin made their ears burn and set their noses to running. They dropped their coats and gloves in a steaming pile near the stove and sat at the table. Veach stretched his legs out and wriggled his toes inside his boots. Had he felt more at home here he would have pulled his boots off so the warmth could reach his feet more quickly.

Ann Waring served them bowls of what looked like faintly discolored water. Veach tried a spoonful of it. It tasted like faintly discolored water. At least it was steaming hot and felt good when the warmth bottomed out in his stomach. He gave Mrs. Waring a smile that he hoped would pass as approval and had another spoonful.

When their bowls were empty — mercifully, Veach thought — he rolled himself a cigarette and offered Waring the tobacco. The man refused it.

"Oh, go ahead. We'll both smoke while we've got it. Later on we can regret our stupidity together and tell each other we shouldn't have squandered it when we had it."

"You really know how to make a man feel better, don't you?" But he accepted the sack and rose to find his pipe. This time, however, he did not pack the brierroot full, using no more of the tobacco than a cigarette would have consumed.

The men were at the table in their shirt sleeves smoking and Ann Waring was curled up on the bed doing something with her fingernails when they heard muffled sounds outside the cabin. Three heads raised simultaneously.

"Hallo, the house," someone called.

The woman was the first to reach her feet. Her eyes were alight with joy, and with relief. "John!" she cried. "Someone made it through after all. We're safe." She flew to the door and yanked it open.

Neither Veach nor her husband was so quick to join her there. They looked at each other with more concern than relief before they moved the few steps to the open doorway where Ann Waring so eagerly stood.

CHAPTER 5

There were two of them, with saddle horses and a pack animal. The men were bulky in heavy coats, their spare trousers on for extra warmth. Hat brims tied down over their ears gave them a hooded, hawklike appearance. The cold made their eyes red and watery above several weeks' growth of dark beard. The combined effect of shadowing hat brim and eye-watering cold made their eyes look like two pairs of coals smoldering in the black ash of a softwood fire. Both men were armed.

They grinned broadly when they saw the woman in the doorway, then nodded to the men who came up behind her.

"G' day, folks," the nearer of them said. When he smiled he exposed a mouthful of yellowed teeth with several gaps where discolored nubs showed above the gum line. "We seen your smoke this mornin'," he said. "Took us all this time to reach ya. Sure will feel good to get by that fire." He pounded gloved hands together and turned to his partner. Without waiting for an invitation he said, "Pull the gear off these horses, Bo, an' dump it in the man's shed. Then rub 'em down before you turn 'em loose, hear? Rub them real good. We don't want them animals taking sick on us like the last ones done. I'll be inside with these nice folks, Bo. You come in an' get warm when you're through."

The second man bobbed his head and turned to the horses. The first waded through the still-deepening snow to the cabin door. He pulled off his right glove and shoved a grimed and heavy-knuckled hand toward Ann Waring. "I'm Jimbo Fyle, little lady. That down there," he hooked a thumb over his shoulder and grinned, "is Bo Jim Hatch. Really that ain't his name. It's really just Jim Hatch, but I took to callin' him Bo, like short for Boy, an' people kinda turned it around so now it's Jimbo and Bo Jim. An' say now, are you folks gonna let me in this little ol' place so's I can snug up to that fire, or ain't you?"

"Yes. Yes, I suppose we should, Mr. Fyle," Waring said. He stepped backward, and Jimbo Fyle shouldered through the doorway.

At a great distance none of them had realized how large the man was, but he nearly filled the doorway passing through it. His bulk was only accented, not caused, by the wolfskin parka he wore. He stood next to the softly purring sheet iron stove and the walls of the tiny cabin seemed scarcely strong enough to contain his presence. He dominated the room merely by standing in it.

Fyle stamped his feet and knocked packed clumps of wet snow to the floor beside the stove. He pulled off his other glove and tossed both onto the table in the center of the room. His hat followed, revealing a shaggy tangle of dark hair long enough to nearly hide the fact that his left ear was missing. He stripped off his steaming parka and handed it to Ann Waring. She had been staring at him in amazed silence, as were her husband and Veach.

"There you go, little lady. Thankee. Sure feels better by this fire, I'll tell you." He scratched himself with no hint of embarrassment, removed his outer pair of trousers and turned his backside to the fire.

Out of his cold-weather garments he gave an impression of even greater size. His height was not very great — slightly less than six feet — but his build was blocky and solid and gave an impression of limitless strength. A vision of a railroad locomotive came to Veach's mind when he looked at Jimbo Fyle — in shape and in physical hardness and in the irresistibility of the man's strength. That strength seemed to flow as much from the overwhelming, battering-ram force of his personality as from his muscles.

Fyle stretched hugely, scratched the ragged beard along his jaw and nodded benignly toward them. "Sure *does* feel good, I tell you. Say now, do you folks have names or are Jimbo an' Bo Jim the only ones willin' to admit to who we are here?" A broad smile remained on his face.

"Yes. Excuse me, Mr. Fyle," Waring said. He introduced the three of them, and Jimbo Fyle shook hands with each, managing to give the impression that he was welcoming them into his presence, that they were the guests here and not he.

Veach shook hands with the man and was surprised on two counts. One, that their eyes were on a level. Jimbo Fyle looked so massive that Veach found it hard to accept that their height was nearly identical. The second surprise was that Fyle's handshake was casual, almost gentle. Veach had expected the man to be a bone crusher. He had prepared himself to feel all the pressure of a smith's vice, but Fyle put none of his great strength into the brief contact. The fact was vaguely disconcerting to Veach, and he eyed Fyle anew when he stepped back away from the man.

Ann Waring seemed disconcerted by him as well. She took a deep breath, then smiled brightly and said, "We are *so* happy to see you, Mr. Fyle. We were afraid we would be trapped here for some time. Now we can all go out together, can't we?"

Fyle threw his head back and rang booming laughter off the stone walls. "Ah, little lady. I sure do hate t' tell you this, 'deed I do, but Jimbo an' Bo Jim are locked in here just the same as you folks. Yes, indeed. We only come three miles down this big ditch since mornin', an' it took us half the day to do that. An' it surely is a fine thing we come on your cabin here, 'cause there's no going out t' the east for a spell now. Judgin' from the tracks we seen, little lady, I'd guess your menfolk already went down an' found that for themselves, didn't you, boys?" He gave his attention to Waring and Veach only long enough to get their affirmative nods. "So you see, little lady, we're all of us going to be here awhile, 'til the weather tells us when we can leave. Sure am sorry to tell you that, but it's a natural fact. No way t' change it."

Jimbo Fyle did not seem to be at all concerned by the fact of their entrapment. He seemed to accept the situation with full confidence that for the time being they were here. Later they would be somewhere else. How or when they would leave did not seem to be of consequence to him. For the time being it was sufficient to be beside the stove with warmth and shelter. He would take tomorrow when it came.

The woman seemed to take some of that confidence from him. She smiled, more genuinely than she had since the snow began, and said, "Then I suppose we may as well make the best of it, Mr. Fyle. Won't you sit down?"

"Why, thankee, little lady." Fyle took the chair nearer the stove and lowered himself into it with unexpected grace.

The door opened with a gush of cold air and Bo Jim came in. He shut the door carefully behind him and tested the latch with his fingertips before he turned to face the room. Even then he did not look around at his new surroundings, but removed his outer clothing and dropped it all into an untidy pile by the door. "Everything's done, Jimbo. Just like you said." He walked to the stove and stood over it, his hands extended palm downward over the top surface.

Bo Jim was somewhat larger than his partner, perhaps three inches taller and just as massively built, yet he did not have anything near the force of Fyle's presence. He was merely a very large man standing beside a stove.

"You rubbed them good, Bo Jim?"

"Yes, I did. Real good."

"You got their legs too?"

"Yes, I did, Jimbo. Real good."

"All right then, Bo Jim. Soon as you get warm you can set over there by the door. An' mind your manners, Bo Jim. Don't you go to staring at the little lady now, you hear?"

"I won't, Jimbo." He rubbed his hands briskly together for only a moment and turned away from the heat of the stove. He walked back to the doorway and ponderously lowered himself onto the cushioning heap formed by his discarded coat and extra trousers. He sat Indian-fashion, not leaning back against the cold stone of the wall. That spot, immediately beside the doorframe, would have been the coldest in the cabin, but Bo Jim gave no sign of discomfort. His face was a blank, and his eyes — Veach could see now that they were oddly pale and almost colorless around pinpoint black pupils — seemed to be focused on no particular place or person before him.

"Bo Jim's a good old boy," Jimbo Fyle said. There was something close to paternal pride in his voice. "I'd trust that ol' boy with my life, folks. Fact is that I've done just that, too, many an' many a time I have. He ain't never once let me down. He's a *real* good boy."

Awareness crossed Bo Jim's features. He looked at Jimbo and beamed his pleasure at the compliment. "Tell 'em about your ear, Jimbo. Please?"

"Ah, these folks don't wanta hear that old story, Bo Jim. Besides, you already know how it turns out." To the Warings and Veach he added, "That's Bo Jim's most favorite story. It's kinda like a kid with a favorite bedtime story, the way he is about it. Bo Jim's kinda like a kid in a lotta ways anyhow. Not that there's anything wrong with him, you understand. He's just kinda different than me an' you folks in some ways."

"You oughta tell 'em about it."

"Not right now, Bo Jim. Another time I will. That's a promise, Bo."

Bo Jim nodded and his face went blank again.

"I really will have to tell you folks about that sometime," Jimbo said. "He's real proud of that story." Fyle rubbed the flat,

72

earless side of his head and laughed. The sound seemed exceptionally loud in the little cabin.

Veach decided he did not particularly want to hear that — or any other — story from Jimbo Fyle, but he felt certain he would hear it sooner or later unless a sudden break in the weather separated them. He was already sure he could practically tell the tale to them rather than hear it from them. It would likely be a long windy, and the odds were strong that it would involve a bear. For some reason such stories always seemed to have a bear in them. Veach doubted that he had ever met a man who had actually touched a live bear. He had heard dozens make claims about wrestling with the creatures.

Sometime, he decided, he would like to meet a man whose tale involved a . . . a wolverine, say. Or a rabid muskrat. Or think how much fun a man could have building one about a horde of enraged ground squirrels. Veach decided that if he ever wanted to go in for windy-making it would be something along those lines.

Waring broke into his reverie by asking Fyle, "I take it you, uh, gentlemen came down from the west then? You were already in the gorge when the snow started?"

"Ayup. We come down yesterday lookin' for the better grass, we did. Not much grazing right around here, you know, an' we seen that bit o' grass an' water down below so we found us a path and come down it." He shook his head. "Sure never counted on this, but then nobody could've figured it." He dismissed it with a wave of his hand. "So anyways, we was settled in for the night, upstream of here, peaceable as anyone could be, an' up come that snow an' wind. Never paid it any mind at first or we'd've gone back up. Didn't seem like such a much at the time. Woke up this mornin' and the sonuvabitch — 'scuse me, little lady — it was plugged, an' then we seen your smoke an' started bucking drifts to get down here to this fire, which surely does feel good." He smiled with genial goodwill at the thought of his present surroundings.

"It must have drifted much worse than I thought upstream if it took you all that time to get here," Waring mused. "If it's that bad above, it must be even worse below us. Worse than I feared."

"Ah well, Johnny. It'll pass. You can take Jimbo's word on that, b'damn. It'll pass whenever it will. Can't change it, man, so jus' set still an' wait it out. Nothin' to worry about, Johnny. Nothing bad ever happens to

Jimbo Fyle."

It was clear the man believed exactly that. Neither man nor nature was going to trouble Jimbo Fyle.

"I hope you're right about that, Mr. Fyle," Ann Waring said lightly. She seemed quite willing to believe him.

"Course I am, little lady. You can take Jimbo's word, whatever he tells you. Indeed you can." He leaned back and slapped his hands heavily on his knees. "Now what do you say we all have a bite to eat, folks? Me an' Bo Jim ain't stopped since we left our cold, dead ashes this mornin', an' I swear I could gag down a raw buzzard, feathers and all, if someone was to hand me one."

The woman looked uncertainly toward her husband. She would be torn between what she knew his wishes to be and the ingrained rules of open-handed hospitality common to her class.

"I'm afraid we're on short rations, Fyle," Waring said quickly, as if afraid his wife would throw open their meager larder to this pair. "We have very little on hand and no way to know how long it has to last. I think it only prudent for us all to get by on as little as possible until the weather breaks and we can be sure of reaching a store or a better prepared homestead than this one."

Fyle laughed. "Prudent, huh? That's a good word, Johnny. B'damn, I got to remember that. But that ol' weather could break tomorra. Then we'd've gone hungry today without no reason. No sir, Johnny." He held up a meaty hand to cut off any protest, even though Waring had not yet ventured any. "I say t'hell with prudent, Johnny. Jimbo an' Bo Jim are hungry now, b'damn. 'Scuse me, little lady." Without turning his head he said, "Bo, you go an' bring our own stuff in. You can have your prudent, Johnny. I'll have m' dinner." With an odd little half-bow he added, "If the little lady there would be good enough t' fix it."

Waring stirred and a faint red flush built in the back of his neck. Veach felt a sympathetic stir of anger himself. The man had no right to come into Waring's home and expect this.

"I'd be glad to, Mr. Fyle," Ann Waring said before the anger could reach her husband's face. She rose and smiled at Bo Jim, who was climbing awkwardly to his feet. "If you would bring in some water, too, I would appreciate it, Mr., uh, Hatch was it?"

Bo Jim grunted. He pulled his coat on and carefully fastened and checked each button to make sure it was secure, then tied his hat in place with the brim down over his ears.

76

He left the cabin. They could hear him fiddling with the latch from the outside to make sure it had caught.

"I'll get your water, Mrs. Waring," Veach said.

"Bo Jim will get it," Fyle answered.

"He didn't take the bucket," Veach persisted.

"I said Bo Jim will get it, an' he will. He just does things in his own time an' his own way. Do you go buttin' in, ol' Bo Jim will get mad now. So stay setting." Fyle gave the impression that it would not be a good thing for Bo Jim to become irritated. Veach remained where he was.

Bo Jim returned a few minutes later with a burlap sack. He stepped inside, placed the sack on the floor, latched the door, picked up the sack and carried it to the table. He did not speak to or appear to look at anyone in the room. He located the water bucket and took it out, once more going through the laborious process of latch-testing from the outside before he walked away.

"You did say the man is different," Veach observed. Jimbo Fyle had ignored Bo Jim while he was in the cabin, but the others had watched him intently the entire time. Had any of the three of them been asked they could not have clearly explained why.

"I also said he's a good ol' boy, now didn't I?" Fyle said lightly. "You can take my word on that too. Jimbo won't tell you no lies." He laughed loudly, as if he had just told a terribly funny joke. When his laughter subsided he upended the sack and tumbled its contents onto the table. "There you go, little lady. You jus' dig in there an' use whatever you want of it. We'll worry about tomorrow when it comes, you hear?" He was obviously feeling expansive, a man distributing largess to more timid souls.

Ann Waring went to the table and surveyed what she found there. Nearly a full bag of coffee. Another containing a large brown lump of sugar. A chunk of smoked bacon. Dried beef. A bag of wheat flour and a battered tin of baking powder.

"Why, I can cook some of this bacon, Mr. Fyle, and with the drippings I can bake some biscuits. How would that be? And coffee? Would that be all right?"

Jimbo Fyle waved his hand airily. "Jus' fine, little lady. Use whatever you want there. Use it all if you like. Hell, I don't care." He scratched his chest and seemed to consider the matter of no further interest.

Bo Jim brought the water in, arranged the door and the bucket to his satisfaction and resumed his seat on the floor. Except for the reddening the renewed warmth brought to his face he might never have left the spot.

Ann Waring hummed softly to herself as she prepared the meal.

CHAPTER 6

Fyle insisted that the others join him and Bo Jim when the meal was ready. They protested, but Veach was glad to have the food when it was pressed upon him, in spite of Ann Waring's lack of ability in preparing biscuits. It was the first solid food he had had that day, and neither mush nor gruel was his idea of a proper meal. He much preferred something that required chewing. Beefsteak — fried leather tough in thick tallow — would be the best, but Fyle's bacon made a most satisfactory substitute.

When they were done Fyle sat back and sighed expansively. "Ah now, that's the way a man oughta feel, right? Belly full an' the stove throwin' heat. The weather be damned is what I say."

"And I, for one, agree with you, Mr. Fyle," the woman said. "I feel *so* much better now. Thank you."

Fyle waved his hand in casual dismissal.

" 'S all right, little lady. An' you set still now. Bo Jim will clean up your dishes here. Won't you, Bo Jim?"

"Sure, Jimbo. I'll clean them good."

Bo Jim left his nest by the doorway and collected the empty plates and soiled forks. The big man absorbed himself in the task of washing, meticulously scrubbing and rinsing and drying each article, one piece at a time.

Veach watched Bo Jim work. He was fascinated by Hatch, although he could not have said why. There was that oddly studied thoroughness with which he seemed to do simple tasks. But he certainly had no nervous mannerisms which would draw attention to him. In fact, Veach wondered if the man had a nerve ending anywhere in his body. He gave an impression of being incapable of impatience.

Perhaps that was it, Veach thought — or part of it. Veach began to realize that in spite of the amount of time he himself had spent among rough men in a roughhewn land, Bo Jim Hatch created within Veach a slow and deep-seated form of fear he had never known before. More dread than fear, really, as of an unknown but totally unrelenting and irresistible force — as if trying to turn Hatch aside from a course he had set

81

himself would be like trying to tear down the mountains or do battle with the snow and ice and cold that now held them all here.

Veach looked at Hatch and involuntarily shuddered. He hoped none of the others had noticed.

"Say now, what're we gonna do to pass the time here, Johnny?" Fyle asked in a loud, cheerful voice. "I don't s'pose you'd have some cards you could break out for a friendly little game?"

Waring shook his head. "No, Mr. Fyle, we are not cardplayers in this house." He gave the man a weak smile. "Besides, we have no money, and I assume you are talking about wagers."

"Not a gamblin' man, Johnny? Now that's a pity. Sure is a pity. But never mind. We'll think of something. Man c'n always use a little rest if he cain't do anything else, right?" He turned in his chair. "Is that right, Bo?"

"It is, Jimbo. You're right."

Fyle nodded his satisfaction with Bo Jim's support. "How 'bout you, Veach? You got some cards maybe and a few dollars you'd care to put up?"

"I'm afraid not," Veach said. "I'm busted near flat, was on my way over to a promised job in the Idaho territory when I got caught in with these nice people. Hit me again in a month and I might have a game with you, though."

Jimbo bounced a roar of laughter off the walls. "Ain't you the optimist all of a sudden. A while ago you was saying we might still be here in a month. Now you figure to be acrost the mountains by then. See what good me an' Bo Jim done for you already? Sure, we got your spirits up now. A bite o' good food an' some pleasant comp'ny an' things be looking better, don't they? Sure it's so."

Fyle got to his feet and took the few steps to the doorway. "Might's well take a look around," he said. He bundled himself into his parka and gloves and stepped outside. The others could see through the briefly opened doorway that the light fall of soft snow continued to drift down.

Even with four people remaining inside, the tiny cabin felt almost empty when Fyle left it. Veach saw Waring's shoulders rise and fall in an unvoiced sigh, and he understood perfectly. Had Bo Jim not been in the room each man would have commented on the feeling. The woman did not appear to notice.

Hatch dried the last fork and laid it gently

onto the shelf where Ann Waring kept her tableware. He had stacked the dishes there and had laid the forks and rearranged the spoons so that each article was lined up exactly perpendicular to the shelf edge, their handles a uniform half inch from the edge. The forks and spoons made a neat, orderly row on the rough wood slab of the shelf. Bo Jim turned away without looking at the others in the room and resumed his seat by the door. He gave no outward signs of awareness that the others existed.

Veach shifted on his chair. He cleared his throat, but did not speak. The things that were on his mind, the things he wanted to discuss with Waring, were not subjects he wanted to bring up in Bo Jim Hatch's presence. Soon he too pushed his chair back and rose. "I think I'll step outside a minute too."

Veach pulled on his coat and gloves and tugged his hat low on his head. In leaving he had to be careful to avoid stepping on Hatch's feet where the man sat cross-legged beside the door, but Bo Jim gave no indication of his passage and did not react to the cold air when the door was pulled open.

The cabin had not felt overly warm, but the brisk, dry air washed over him when he stepped into it. There was a pleasant, stove-hollow warmth in his belly where the solid food and hot coffee lay like a clutch of buried coals. He felt the heat of it inside him even as wispy fingers of frigid air crept beneath his coat. He shivered slightly, but the contrasting sensations were not unpleasant.

Fyle's footprints led off to the left toward the livestock shed, and Veach automatically moved along them, following the disturbed snow where Fyle had walked before him.

Jimbo Fyle, he saw, had clambered up a shaky rick of piled wood and was standing on the shed roof. The man had a pair of field glasses and was studying the gorge upstream from the cabin. He apparently heard the faint crunch of snow being compacted beneath Veach's boots, for he lowered the glasses and turned.

Veach thought he saw a brief flicker of apprehension on Jimbo's face, but he decided he must have been mistaken. Fyle smiled gaily and waved a gloved hand westward.

"I keep hopin' we was wrong," Jimbo said, "but I sure don't see nothing that direction. Fact is, I wonder we got through some of them drifts as it is. Wanta look?"

Veach shook his head. "No point in it. Waring said it's seventeen miles to the nearest good path up in that direction."

"Is that a fact? Be damned if it seemed that far. Course we was mostly ridin' in good weather comin' down here. Never paid it no mind how far we'd come. Sure never seemed that far." He tucked the glasses into a leather case slung around his neck and carefully negotiated the lumpy, snow-padded dirt roof of the shed. He lowered himself over the edge of the pole roof and scrambled agilely down to the ground. "Nothin' the other way either," he said.

"No, we checked that pretty well this morning."

"D'you check the trail on that other wall too?"

"We didn't go over to it, no."

Fyle squinted across the gorge. He seemed to be paying more attention to the high rim than to the ice-and-snow-covered path leading down from it. "Not much point, I wouldn't reckon."

"No."

The animals were all beneath that wall, the four horses grouped together below the foot of the path and the three mules paying into the snow upstream from them. They looked bleakly alone against the stark white snow and black rock of the gorge.

Fyle chuckled merrily to himself. He seemed quite amused by something.

"What?" Veach asked.

"Huh?"

"What's so funny that you're standing there laughing to yourself?"

"Was I now? Yeah, well, I was just thinkin' that me an' Bo Jim are havin' such a run of good luck, you see. Us findin' this here place so unexpected. Cozy warm an' snug away from the wind an' snow, see. Good lo— good woman like Waring's ole lady t' do the cookin'. Yessir, I was just thinking that that right there is plain good luck, I was. Why, a fella caught out in the open might could have himself some real trouble now, 'specially if he hadn't thought to carry much in the way of food. Fella could starve hisself, he could, an' if he hadn't no ax or saw he might even manage to freeze hisself stiff as a pine log. Not thaw out 'til spring, maybe. Yessir, that's what I'd be thinkin'."

Veach shivered again. The dinner warmth in his belly had nearly left him now and he was starting to feel the cold. Soon he would have to go back inside or start moving to build some heat in his muscles. "That doesn't seem any too funny to me," he said.

"Ah, but it is now, Veach, 'cause me an' Bo Jim ain't in that kinda sitty-ation, don't you see? That's what makes it such a thing for the laughin' and the enjoyin'." He gave

Veach a broad, delighted smile.

"Still and all, I'd be happier if this would break soon." He stamped his feet and said, "I think I'll go over and take a look at that path anyhow."

Jimbo looked at it again and craned his neck to look up at the near wall rim hanging high above them. "I might's well walk along."

Veach nodded and cut down toward the thin stream. The snow was not yet deep enough on the open, flat ground to present a problem, but its depth was enough to annoy and to drag at their feet, making the act of walking an effort that pulled unfamiliarly at knees and thighs more used to horseback travel. The horses eyed their approach with suspicion and moved aside as the men came near.

The base of the path was buried in a small drift of loose snow, but Veach kicked the drift apart and was pleased to find rough rock beneath, unhindered by ice glaze. Cautiously he climbed a few yards to the thinner accumulation of more recent snow that would have fallen after the wind died. It was here that Waring's knowledge was confirmed. The rock was treacherously iced. Veach attempted only once to step onto the path above the protection of the drift snow.

His boot slipped almost immediately and he caught himself with a heart-pounding lurch.

"Damn!" he yelped. In trying to steady himself he had flailed wildly out with his right hand and smashed his wrist against unyielding, frozen rock.

Fyle laughed. "Not so easy, huh?"

Veach rubbed his wrist for a moment and quietly cursed both himself and Jimbo Fyle. "Worse than it looks, even." He turned and started gingerly downward. "Watch out I don't come sailing off of here and light on you."

Fyle laughed again, but moved a few steps back. He had not tried to follow Veach onto the path. Veach came down and stood for a minute, glad to have level earth underfoot again. The slip had startled and disturbed him, even though it had taken place low enough so that a fall probably would have done little harm.

Jimbo Fyle pulled his field glasses from the case and began sweeping the opposite rim, above the cabin. A thin thread of spreading smoke bisected the towering rock wall. The pale smoke stood out in sharp contrast against the rock, but was lost to sight against the gray sky above the rim.

"If there was a way up over there, Waring

would know of it," Veach said.

Fyle grunted a response but continued to sweep the full length of the rim before he replaced the glasses. "Reckon he would at that," the man said cheerfully.

"Well, I don't know about you, but I'm getting kind of cold. I think I'll go see if there's any coffee left."

"Say now, fella, that sounds like a fine idea, it does. Let's you an' me go get some of that, an' if there ain't any made, why, we'll just have the little lady boil us up some fresh. Yessir, that'd go real good now." Fyle led the way back across the deepening flat.

CHAPTER 7

The second boiling of the grounds tasted nearly as good as the first, Veach decided. He wrapped his hands gratefully around the mug Ann Waring handed him. The heat from the coffee cut through the chill in his fingers and for a moment he luxuriated in the sensation of holding something that was really too hot to touch. Quickly, then, he set the mug on the table before him.

The seating pattern in the cabin seemed firmly established already. The Warings perched on the edge of their bunk. Fyle lounged in the chair nearer the stove. Veach noticed for the first time that from there Fyle could observe everyone in the room and the closed doorway as well. And Bo Jim Hatch sat cross-legged beside the door. Veach had given his own chair a half turn so he could shift his attention between the Warings and Fyle. His back was toward Hatch, but he doubted that the big man would have noticed that; much less did he expect that Hatch would have minded.

It was already nearly dark outside, the snow-laden cloud cover and taller mountain formation to the west combining to bring on a premature nightfall, and Veach began wondering about the sleeping positions they would take. In a spurt of irrational pique, he wondered if Jimbo Fyle was going to usurp the stove-side place Veach had occupied the night before. Veach had no more right to claim territory within the cabin than Fyle did, but Fyle had already shown himself to be pushily presumptuous and Veach was prepared to be angry about it when the expected took place.

They drank their coffee in silence. No one seemed to have anything to say, not even Ann Waring, although a scant twenty-four hours earlier she had been ecstatic over the prospect of having a visitor. Veach wondered if Bo Jim Hatch's silently indifferent but somehow pervasive presence was putting a damper on her spirits. And it had been some time now since she had had any opportunity to speak privately with her husband — or to have any other form of privacy, he realized. The matter of simple privacy could become an awkward thing for them all, but for the woman far more than the men.

When they were done with the coffee Jimbo Fyle set his mug aside and said, "Bo, I think we'll be needing more water now. You c'n fetch that an' some more wood. An' mind you take a good look around while you're outside. If you see anything that needs shooting you come an' get me, hear?"

"I will, Jimbo. I'll look real careful." He climbed heavily to his feet, bent to retrieve his crushed and weight-crumpled coat and bundled himself against the cold. He left without taking the water bucket again.

"What in the world could need shooting out there?" Veach asked idly when the man was gone.

"Ah now, you just never know, fella. Might be a deer could wander down or some such thing. It ain't real likely, but it might could happen. An' to tell you the truth of it, does something happen by, I wouldn't want ol' Bo Jim to try an' shoot it hisself. He's an awful fine boy, Bo Jim is, but he's the damnedest — 'scuse me, little lady — he's the damnedest, poorest shot I think I ever did see. I don't think that boy could hit the horse he was riding. Sure couldn't bring in meat for the pot. Say now, little lady, you'd be willin' to do some fancy cooking, wouldn't you, if we was to fetch in a fat doe or some such edible?" He smiled genially at

93

the woman and seemed to have dismissed Hatch from his mind.

When she nodded Fyle grinned and launched himself into a lengthy accounting of game he had killed and how he liked wild meat to be prepared. He had a number of fixed opinions on the subject.

"I don't think it very likely that he would find game down here," Waring said when Fyle finally ran down. "They haven't been using this trail since we moved in and certainly couldn't start now. If you saw none upstream there could be none here now."

"Well now, Johnny, you just never know," Fyle responded. "Me an' Bo Jim broke trail comin' down here, and one just might've used that path, you see." He expounded on the unpredictability of wildlife and cited several unlikely-sounding examples from his own experience. By the time he was done Hatch was back with a large load of wood.

Bo Jim opened the door, picked up the wood from the snow outside, brought it in and set it on the floor where he had been sitting earlier. He seemed unmindful of the clinging snow that fell to the floor and began to melt there. He closed and tested the latch carefully before he moved the stove-lengths to the woodbox.

"I looked all around, Jimbo," he reported.

"Nothing moving. I was real careful."

"That's good, Bo. You did just fine."

Bo Jim gave Jimbo a broad, rare smile in gratitude for the compliment. He took the water bucket and left again. He was back in a few moments that time. When he removed his coat he dropped it on top of the partially melted snow beside the door. Once seated his expression and his position were such that he might not have moved from the spot for hours.

Bo Jim must have felt heartened by the compliment, though, for after a few minutes he asked, "Jimbo, why don't you tell them about your ear now, huh?"

Fyle gave him a benign, paternal smile and said, "All right, Bo, I'll just do that thing." Ignoring Hatch then, he turned to the others and shrugged. "Like I told you folks, that's his most favorite story. He's awful proud of it."

He leaned back in his chair and took a deep breath. "This was a little better'n three years ago, you see. Before me an' Bo Jim tied in together. I was doin' some business over in Nevada. Just come over from the California side an' I didn't know a soul anywheres in the territory right at first.

"Well anyhow, I had me a little poke and got into a game of, uh, chance an' put a bit

95

more into my poke. Got myself liquored up good an' proper, I did, for I was having me some fun. You know how it is. The little lady there prob'ly don't know about such things," he said with a polite nod in her direction, "but that's the way menfolk will do when they're flush an' having a high time of it. Old Bo Jim — he was called Jim then an' didn't know me so good as he does now — he was in the game too, an' he come out of it a loser. Took him for every last cent he had, I did, an' then I bought him a snort or two to show I was bein' a gent about it, which I always like t' be, you see. Always leave a fella feelin' good after you do business with him is the way I look at it. If he gives you any choice about it, anyways. I've always felt that way about things. Hope I always will." For some reason the others did not understand this prompted him to boom a peal of laughter off the roof.

Veach decided he had been mistaken after all. He did not see how Fyle was going to work a bear into this story.

"Anyway," Jimbo went on, "me an' Bo Jim had a drink or two, an' I reckon he was thinking I can't hold my likker as good as I can. Ain't that right, Bo?"

Hatch smiled shyly and bobbed his head in agreement. The man was listening now with rapt attention. As indifferent as he had been before, he now was focused wholly on Jimbo Fyle and the much-favored story.

"So what happened," Fyle said, "was that we went out toward the, uh, backhouse, and ol' Bo decided he'd just take back his money an' take mine too, you see. Well, he come down on me like a barrel fallin' onto an eggshell. He thought he did, anyhow. He just figured he had it all wrapped up, don't you see.

"Well, to make a long story short, we had us some kind of a tussle there in the dark. We punched and gouged and commenced to kicking, and pretty soon we was both bloody as a pair of shoats at butchering time. Me, I was near to wore out, and ol' Bo, he knocked me down flat on my back. Well, I kicked him one in the kneecap — between bein' tired and bein' drunk I wasn't kicking so accurate right then — an' he fell smack on top of me. Busted a couple of ribs and knocked the air clean out of me so I couldn't get my breath to going right again for a while.

"Ol' Bo thought he had 'er made then. He commenced to choking me, an' I put a knee into him an' made a few passes at his eyes, an' damned if that ol' boy didn't duck his head and clomp down on my ear. My oh my, folks, but that boy there c'n *bite,* I'm here to tell you. First thing you know he had ripped my ear clean off from my head. Spit it out in the dirt, he did. Hurt something terrible, too, I can tell you.

"But what he also done was to get me mad. So I jus' naturally got up from there an' beat the pure hell out o' that boy — 'scuse me, little lady, but that's the politest way to say what I done. Left that boy in some *kind* of bad shape, don't you see." Fyle looked expectantly at Bo Jim.

The larger man grinned hugely. "That was the first time anybody'd ever whupped me," he said.

"The last, too," Fyle added. "An' I'd sure hate to have to do 'er again, I can tell you. Anyway, the upshot of the whole thing was that Bo took a likin' to me after that. Started followin' me around town like a pup, an' we been together ever since, haven't we, Bo?"

Bo Jim nodded happily.

"What's more, the next day he dragged hisself back to that alley an' found my ear for me."

"We tried to pickle it," Bo Jim said, "but I guess I done something wrong. Part of it rotted. So I dried what was left." He fished inside the neck of his shirt and drew out a leather pouch suspended there by a stout thong. With great care his thick, blunt fingers plucked at the drawstring and pulled the mouth of the pouch open. He dipped inside it and produced a dried and twisted thing that looked like a scrap of leather from a saddler's floor sweepings. "Jimbo let me keep it," he said proudly.

Bo Jim climbed heavily to his feet and carried Jimbo Fyle's ear to each of the others. He handled it gently, with almost a reverent deference, the way the devout might handle a sanctified relic. It was quite obviously his most precious possession.

"Yeah, me an' Bo Jim been together ever since," Jimbo said. His tone expressed pride in Bo Jim for the accomplishment of the fight. "An' we make a good team, too. Haven't never had the first argument since the day we partnered."

" 'N I wouldn't argue with Jimbo, neither. He's the only man could ever whup me, but he sure did it real good. Real good." Bo Jim tenderly replaced Jimbo Fyle's dried ear in its pouch and resumed his seat by the door. His face did not immediately return to its usual blank indifference, however. The faint afterglow of a smile lingered there for some time.

Fyle nodded to himself several times. "Good ol' boy, Bo Jim is," he muttered.

No, Veach thought to himself, I could not complain about that being just another bear-wrestling story.

CHAPTER 8

John Waring rubbed his eyes and appeared to be deep in thought once again — as much still as again, really, for he had been the same way all afternoon — and Veach could not blame him. If the man had had cause to feel troubled before, his concern was doubly valid now.

His worry should be all the more acute after hearing Jimbo Fyle's story of that brawl and the way Hatch maimed the man while trying to rob him. Fyle had made no pretense that the fight was about anything else. He had seemed to find nothing exceptional in the action. Veach wondered if Fyle was as casually unlawful in his outlook as Hatch apparently was.

Their presence now would add all the more burden to Waring's concern. His fears would be not so much about the food they would require or the inconvenience they would cause; he would have the newly added concern that when the weather did break, tomorrow or the next week or a month in the future, traveling in their company might be dangerous if they learned what Waring's packs would hold. Veach had seen enough already to guess that Waring would have a sizable amount tucked away somewhere in the cabin. His knowledge was bad enough; Waring did not know him well enough to trust him either. But it would be clearly suicidal to let Jimbo Fyle and Bo Jim Hatch learn of Waring's work here. The merest hint to either of them might be enough to turn the cabin into a medieval chamber of horrors. Waring could not know for sure that this would be so, but he could take no chances, not as long as his woman was confined here with them. Veach was glad the problem was not his. It was bad enough having to share an outsider's portion of it.

John Waring groaned faintly from the depth of his worry and looked startled when his wife asked, "Are you all right, dear?" He did not seem to realize he had uttered the sound aloud. "Yes, of course. Fine. Why do you ask?"

"I . . . nothing. Never mind." She shook her head.

Still looking puzzled, Waring gave her a

reassuring smile and brought his attention back to the others in the tiny room. He sighed.

Waring rose and crossed to the doorway, having to nearly step on Hatch when he leaned forward to pull the door a few inches ajar and peer outside. Hatch made no effort to move aside, did not in any way so much as acknowledge Waring's presence standing over him. Waring pushed the door to and turned back to face the room.

"It's nearly dark already," he announced. The others had already long since noticed the premature nightfall. "I think we, uh, should all step outside for a few minutes, gentlemen. Mrs. Waring will need some privacy to prepare herself for sleep."

Veach nodded quickly and came to his feet. He began bundling himself into his coat. Fyle rubbed his chin for a moment. He seemed lost in thought. At length he nodded. "All right," he said. "Could get t' be a nuisance if the weather goes much colder, though. C'mon, Bo."

The men filed out into the cold darkness.

The temperature was definitely dropping again, and the snowfall had lightened. The flakes were harder and smaller than they had been during the day, but now they were not wind-driven. The flakes fell plumb-bob straight from the low cloud cover.

Jimbo Fyle tipped his hat back and peered up at the dimly visible sky. He uttered a coarse oath and stamped his boots in the snow. "Looks like the clouds is breakin' up for sure," he said. "I don't much like that, b'damn."

Veach and Waring shook their heads in agreement with him and also gave the sky an inspection. It looked to Veach, too, as if the sky was clearing slightly. He hoped it would not. Continued light winds might have carried a warming chinook off the Pacific when the cold front passed. If the sky cleared the temperature would plummet. It might well remain that way — bright and still and icily cold — for a long time.

Jimbo Fyle grinned at Bo Jim. He laughed out loud and scratched himself. "Ah well," he said, "there's worse things could happen. Whatever comes, we'll just ride 'er out, won't we, Bo?" He laughed again. "There's nothin' bad ever happens to Jimbo. No sir, nothin' bad at all."

Veach wondered briefly if Fyle's self-proclaimed hold on good fortune extended to those around him. He rather hoped it did.

"I suppose we should bring in the live-stock," Waring said.

"Naw, leave 'em be," Fyle objected. "Does it turn cold they're gonna need all they can rustle to keep them fit. Hell, they cain't go off nowhere anyhow. An' if they did I'd say good. We could follow 'em out if they found a way."

"I lost some mules to predators," Waring said. "I don't know that they would be safe in the open at night."

Fyle snorted. "Nothin's coming down here in this weather, Johnny." His voice turned harder. "Anyhow, I said we leave 'em out. That's what we'll do." He seemed to find no inconsistency in his statements earlier about looking for wild meat and his denial now that predators could reach them.

Waring nodded pleasantly. His expression was mildly inoffensive, but his pale eyes were unwavering when he looked at the much larger man. "Good enough, Mr. Fyle. Your horses can remain outside. I'll bring my mules in, though." He began wading through the snow toward the far wall where the animals were faint shadows visible against the snow.

"I'll give him a hand," Veach said. He wondered when he did if some division had been reached among the occupants of the cabin. Reached . . . or merely reaffirmed.

Waring heard the soft crunch of snow being packed beneath Veach's boots behind him. He stopped to wait for the man. "Will you be bringing your horse in too?"

"Uh-huh, I reckon," Veach said. "It won't hurt to play it safe. Besides, if we have to be here any length of time it might be better to limit the amount of grazing these animals do. Once it's gone, that's all she wrote for a while."

"Yes, I thought of that too. There seems little point in asking Fyle for prudence, though."

They walked on, the snow dragging at their legs and the cold quickly invading the leather of their boots. Together they cut Veach's horse away from the others, then hazed him and the mules back toward the rock shelter. The mules were accustomed to the overnight confinement and the horse joined them readily, following them inside without trying to break back toward the other horses.

Fyle and Hatch were hunkered beside the woodpile, Fyle with a belt knife and pocket-sized whetstone in his hands. Neither of them spoke while Waring and Veach put the animals in and fitted the poles across the shed opening.

"It's gettin' damn cold out here, Johnny," Fyle said when they were done. "You reckon your woman's had time enough to finish her business now?" There was a faint but definite edge of annoyance in his voice.

Waring disregarded the undertone and smiled. "I'll see if she has, Mr. Fyle." He went inside and reappeared a moment later carrying a crockery slop jar. "Go on inside, gentlemen. I'll join you in a moment." He disappeared around the downstream end of the cabin.

Fyle returned his knife to its sheath and carefully wrapped a scrap of rag around his stone before he dropped it into a pocket. "Let's get ourselves warm, Bo," he said as he came fluidly to his feet. He ignored Veach.

The three men reentered the small cabin, Jimbo Fyle leading the way, the far less gracefully moving Bo Jim Hatch at his heels. Veach trailed behind them.

The makeshift curtain of blankets was closed, screening the bunk from view and making the cabin seem much smaller. Ann Waring was not in sight, although an occasional rope-creak could be heard from the bunk. The woman was not yet asleep.

They stripped off their coats and gloves. Hatch resumed his seat beside the door. Fyle scratched himself contentedly and stood beside the stove. He pulled the firebox door open and shoved in more split stove-lengths. Veach noticed that the woodbox was already showing the inroads being made on it by the need for constant refueling.

Waring returned and shoved the slop jar beneath the hanging edge of one of the blankets. He turned and looked pensively around the crowded cabin while he removed his coat and muffler.

"Veach," Waring said, "would you mind spreading your blankets on this side of the table?" He motioned along the narrow strip of dirt floor between the table and the Warings' bunk. "Mr. Fyle, I suggest you bed down between the table and the stove. And Mr. Hatch in front of the door."

Fyle grunted as if he thought the arrangement obvious — as if he would not have considered sleeping anywhere but in the most favored position by the stove.

Veach stifled a surge of irritation. He looked at Waring and at the blanket that would loom above Veach's bedding through this and the nights to follow. With the floor space so severely limited one of them had to be there. Putting Veach there merely meant that Waring trusted him more than Fyle or Hatch. The man did not want either of them so close to Ann Waring.

Veach sighed and got his bedroll from the

corner where he had tucked it that morning. It had been a long day, he decided, and far from a pleasant one — on several counts. He hoped the morrow would be better.

CHAPTER 9

Veach was a long time getting to sleep. During the day, especially after the appearance of Jimbo Fyle and Bo Jim Hatch, he had been too busy, his thoughts too intently concentrated on other things, to even be consciously aware of the remembered images that now flashed through his thoughts. All of those images centered on Ann Waring.

Lying in the stove-flicker-softened darkness, alone on his blanket spread across hard earth floor, Veach had an unexpected recollection of such clarity that he was made uncomfortable by the implications that it might have. He could see with absolute precision the slender column of the woman's neck, smoothly sculpted along the delicate lines of her throat as she had turned her head to look toward the front of the cabin from her accustomed seat on the bunk — the same bunk that now was so close above and beside him. He could remember the scene exactly. Every contour in the hollow of her throat. The fine-grained mat texture of her skin there. The lamp-warmed coloration, pale yet so entirely appropriate to the fine texture.

Again he could see in his mind the woman's hand as she placed a cup of coffee on the table before him that afternoon. A small hand, the fingers long and pencil slim, a faintly seen tracery of veins visible beneath the skin, tendon lines rising and shifting with the flex of her fingers. He had not noticed her nails at the time, but now he remembered them. A jarring note amid delicacy, the nails were short, bitten and torn into red-rimmed nubs layered at the tips with yet-to-be-peeled flakes. It was odd, he thought, that he had not noticed her biting or picking at her nails, yet she obviously did so. He was certain that his recollection was accurate. And he was equally sure that they had not been so when he first saw her.

He could remember her face as she listened at one point to Jimbo Fyle's flow of confident talk. Interest expressed in a slight forward tilt of her head, head cocked ever so slightly to the left, a tiny ringlet of pale silvery-yellow hair curling forward of her right ear, the ear itself small and curved and with a thin translucence that gave it an almost brittle, porcelain appearance, a hint of tightening around large, dark eyes, lashes curled but not fluttering as her attention and her gaze were fixed on the man across the room. The same cream-smooth skin texture on her face as at the throat. An appearance of velvet softness. Veach ran the tip of his tongue across his lips and imagined he knew what the scent and the flavor of her skin would be.

Another image arose: the tiny span of her waist with rounded fullness swelling above and below. In his memory he saw her bending at the woodbox, hips and derriere toward the table where he sat. He saw her twisting away from the stove to answer a question, the fabric of her dress pulled taut against the high, firm breasts of youthful womanhood.

But it was her husband's question she had turned to answer. A husband who was a good and a decent man and who did not deserve to have his wife inspected, even admiringly, especially admiringly, like livestock at auction.

Veach gnawed his lower lip and twisted beneath his blanket. The dirt was unyielding under him and at that moment he was glad it gave him no comfort. He felt he deserved none. He lay awake, sweating lightly, and could not will himself to ignore the sounds of slumberous breathing that came from the bunk above him. The woman was asleep. He could hear that plainly in her breathing. He could hear as plainly that Waring was not. Veach was positive of the identification based solely on the sounds of gentle breathing. Across the room he could also hear Bo Jim Hatch breathing heavily in sleep. Of Fyle he had heard nothing. He, too, would be awake then. With a flush of annoyance Veach wondered about Jimbo Fyle's night thoughts. He resentfully speculated that they might be all too close to his own.

Veach sat up and fumbled in his shirt pocket for his tobacco and papers. He could sense Fyle stirring on the other side of the table, but the man did not openly signal his wakefulness or otherwise invite conversation. Veach rolled his cigarette. He twisted the ends and thought about saving a match by going around the table to the still-burning stove, but decided against it. He did not want to talk with Fyle at the moment either. He thumbed one of his few matches alight and drew gratefully on the smoke. He heard Waring stir on the other side of the hung blankets.

For a time Veach sat cross-legged on his blankets, smoking and staring toward the darkness of the front cabin wall where Hatch was sleeping. The man began to snore.

The fire in the stove was already burning low, and Veach could feel a chill beginning to form at floor level. By morning he would be wishing he had more blankets, he knew. For the moment, though, the cabin was still comfortable. He shivered, but more in anticipation than discomfort.

He ground the cigarette out on the dirt floor and rubbed his forehead. He had a mild headache that he attributed to the closeness of the cabin. With so many people occupying the space it seemed even smaller. Veach could smell — or imagined he could smell — the heavy man-scents common to barracks and hotel tents and the other places where men who seldom bathed gathered for sleep. He had noticed no such odors earlier, and he wondered whether the night brought them on or only made him aware of them. And the smallness of the cabin had not bothered him before. Now it did. Now, in the darkness, he felt too closely confined. He wished he could slip outside for a deep lungful of crisp, clean air. Had Hatch not been sleeping across the doorway he would have done so.

With a sigh Veach lay back down and tried to force his thoughts beyond John Waring's cabin and the weather that held them all here. He tried to think instead about the lights and the attractions of the camp where his job was supposed to be waiting. Nevertheless it was some time before he slept, and his thoughts until then were not all pleasant ones. And some were far too pleasant.

Veach woke up with a hollow ache in his lower belly that had nothing to do with the hunger pangs that rumbled and gurgled higher in his stomach. He rolled face down on his blanket and listened. The others were beginning to restlessly move also.

There was no light inside the cabin and no way to tell if the sky was growing lighter outside. Somehow he did not think it was yet.

The inside of the cabin was cold, almost bitterly so, in spite of the collected body heat of the five people sleeping there. Their exhalations seemed only to have added to the humidity so that the cold cut bone deep now. Veach shivered and reached backward over his shoulder to pull the rough wool of his blanket snug around his ears. In practice the effort seemed good more as a gesture than for any actual benefit.

Off to the side he could hear the muffled sound of another blanket being moved and a moment later the metallic clank of the firebox latch as Jimbo Fyle groped for it in the darkness. The sharp tapping of metal on metal seemed unnaturally loud in the deep silence of the snow-covered cabin.

Fyle looked in and saw the welcome red glow of ash-hidden coals in the bottom of the stove. By touch he located a handful of split wood from the box nearby and used the end of one stick to uncover the coals remaining from the night fire. He positioned the smallest sticks carefully and within moments was rewarded with a growing lick of bright flame that soon flooded the inside of the firebox with light that spilled out into the room as well. When the new fire was well caught he added fuel and, heedless of the noise, shook the grate to dump the last night's ash so the fire could draw freely. He stuffed the firebox with heavier wood and shortly had to move away from the intense heat radiating from the sheet metal. The walls of the stove creaked and popped as the metal expanded. Fyle left the door open for the light it threw into the room.

Bo Jim Hatch sat up, yawning and rubbing his face. He let his blankets fall to his waist unnoticed. Hatch did not shiver or give any outward indication of discomfort, although his was the coldest place in the cabin. He yawned again and scratched his chest.

Ropes creaked in protest and the grass mattress rattled quietly behind the blanket screen across the Waring bunk. One of the blankets jerked eerily in the faint light from the firebox and John Waring's bare feet shoved into view between the two blankets of the screen. The man stepped on Veach's hip and quickly snatched his foot away with a sleep-thickened mumble of apology.

The others could hear the woman muttering, half awake and searching for her husband's warmth no longer pressed against her on the small bed they shared. Veach was achingly aware of her presence so close to his blankets. He heard her shift across the bed, trying to nuzzle against Waring like a pup seeking the comfort-making nearness of its dam. At that moment Veach was glad the cabin was so poorly lighted by the fire in the open stove.

Veach hunkered at the table edge and rolled his blankets quickly to pull them out of Waring's way. He tossed the wadded blankets against the back wall and raised himself into the chair.

Waring nodded and stood, letting the blankets fall back into place between the bunk and the visitors in his home. There had been too little light and too narrow an opening for any of them to have looked at Ann Waring in her bed.

"Ah now, Johnny. A lovely morning to you," Fyle said cheerfully. He, at least, was fully awake now.

Waring grunted what might have been a greeting and stood swaying on unsteady legs. He hunched his shoulders against the chill and pushed a spill of hair back away from his eyes.

Fyle laughed with quick delight at Waring's morning grogginess. "Might as well face it, Johnny-boy. You can't run from the dawning." He grinned broadly. "Though I've tried an' I've tried a time or two."

Jimbo Fyle grew more serious at some thought that he did not share with the others. He turned to Hatch and said, "Bo, go take a look around the place. Mind that you check real good for tracks now. Somethin' might've come down durin' the night, so look close. If you see anything come tell me."

Hatch nodded and came ponderously to his feet. He had slept fully clothed, including his boots. He pulled on his coat and gloves and left. The light showing through the briefly opened doorway was still water thin.

"We might as well all go out and get to feeling more, uh, comfortable after the night," Veach said. He bent to tug his boots on.

"In a minute," Fyle snapped. There was a hard and unmistakable edge of command in his tone.

Veach paused, a finger still hooked in the mule-ear of his right boot, and looked up at Fyle. Their eyes locked in the near darkness. "Why the hell should we wait, Fyle?" he demanded, forgetting for the moment the presence of the woman immediately behind him.

Fyle's chin rose menacingly. It was clear that he did not like to have his judgment questioned on this or any other subject, but after only a fraction of a moment he smiled and said, "Because you jus' never know, Veach. Some ol' deer or something might've come a-tumbling down last night. Wouldn't do t' scare it off with too many people stomping around an' stirring up a fuss. We'll just give Bo Jim a minute for his look-see an' then we can all go out. Let the little lady have her privacy an' all that. Sound reason-

119

able to you, fella?"

It did not, but Veach shrugged. He could not see what Fyle was so insistent about. In the unlikely event some wild animal had fallen to where they could reach it, the creature could not get away from them — not without showing them a way out themselves. And with a thick pad of snow on the ground a troop of cavalry could parade up and down the flat without raising dust or enough noise to frighten the most sensitive of game animals. Still, it did not seem important enough to quarrel over. He finished pulling his boots on and got his coat and hat from the wall.

Waring too dressed and got his coat, ready to leave but waiting patiently. In a few minutes Hatch opened the door and stuck his head in. "Nothing going on, Jimbo. Nothing at all."

"Go on back out, Bo. We'll be right along," Fyle ordered. "Now, fella, let's step outside an' give the little lady some relief." From his tone it seemed he had appropriated the idea as his own. He sounded quite solicitous toward Ann Waring's comfort.

Veach nodded, and he and Fyle left the tiny cabin, just beginning to grow warm. Waring lingered behind them, although not for long.

CHAPTER 10

The sky was clear, with no remaining trace of the leaden clouds that had hung overhead the evening before. A few morning stars showed pale and unwavering between the high gorge walls. The snowfall had stopped sometime during the night without adding greatly to the previous accumulation.

The temperature was somewhere on the minus side of the scale. They had no gauge, but as soon as he stepped outside Veach could feel the hairs in his nose freeze into uncomfortable, spiky needles, and the snow squeaked shrilly under their boots. The hard cold had come in as they had feared it might, and there was no sign of the moving weather that would be required to sweep it away.

Veach visibly shuddered in his concern. If anyone noticed he hoped it would have been taken for a shiver instead.

Fyle tilted his head back to view the clear

sky. "Could be worse, boys," he said. "Uh-huh. Damn sure could be. At least we ain't having to put up with no damned blizzard. Does it come a chinook now, why, this li'l bit of snow could be gone and away in a few hours' time. Even the drifts won't lay long once the warm wind comes blowin' down through here."

Waring came out and pulled the door closed behind him. "I wish I was that optimistic, Fyle," he said. He squinted unhappily upward at the clear and now brightening sky. "Something like this could stay for a long time. Too long."

"Don't worry yourself about it, Johnny. Hear now? No need t' worry. We could get us a little ol' warm-up any time. Meantime we can rest our weary ol' bones, right?" Fyle was smiling easily, his eyes bright and cheery. He seemed genuinely unaffected by concern.

"Well," Veach said, "whether we have reason to worry or we don't, we can't change it anyway. And the animals need to be let out of the shed, Waring."

Their host looked nervously up and down the bleak, snow-locked gorge floor. The three horses belonging to Fyle and Hatch were huddled against the far wall, steam rising from their backs and jetting from their nostrils. "Of course," Waring said absently.

Waring trailed Veach to the rock shelter, while Fyle and Bo Jim Hatch turned the other way, trudging out of sight through the crusty snow at the downstream end of the cabin.

Waring glanced over his shoulder as Veach lifted the bars down from the mouth of the shed and hazed the mules and one horse outside.

"I don't mind telling you, Veach," he said when he was sure neither Fyle nor Hatch was near, "I'm not altogether comfortable with those men. I gave this some thought last night — quite a bit of thought — and I want to ask you a rather direct question if you don't mind."

Veach was standing with his arms folded, watching the newly released animals swing across the gorge floor in a head-high trot toward the other horses. He grunted and turned to face Waring. "Ask it then."

"Last night, that business with the horses . . . I believe our Mr. Fyle could be a very difficult person if he were not getting his way. And frankly I don't trust him. You, uh, know certain things about the . . . situation of my wife and myself here, Mr. Veach." He paused and looked inquiringly at the taller man.

"I know what you're saying, Waring. So what?"

"What I wanted to ask, you see, if I may be blunt about it, is simply this. If it comes to a, uh, division among us, Mr. Veach, can I count on your help?"

Veach turned his head toward the animals and stood for a moment with his eyes unfocused. He was not so much thinking about the question as he was letting it sink in for that period. He puffed his cheeks out and exhaled loudly. "Well now, John, you did say you were gonna be direct about it, didn't you?"

"Yes," Waring said quietly. Now that he had brought the matter into the open between himself and Veach he seemed at ease with it.

"I'll tell you this way, John. I won't go along with anybody, not them nor you either, doing anything that isn't right. If that means taking sides, well, I'll do what I think is right when the time comes. But if your real question is whether I'm going to tell those boys about what you have stashed here, now I'm not going to do a thing like that. And I guess it would make me kind of hot was you to suggest that I might." He locked his eyes on Waring's.

The man smiled. "I made no such suggestion, Mr. Veach. Nor will I do so in the future." He hesitated. "Thank you."

Veach shrugged. "No need."

"Still, I do appreciate it, and I'm glad now that I brought it up. The truth is that I've been more than a little concerned."

"I guess I can't blame you for that, you and your missus being thrown in with a bunch of people you never saw before. But hell, man, maybe old Jimbo is right. Maybe this will break today and we can all ride out of here tomorrow."

"Mr. Veach, you don't believe that any more than I do."

Veach grinned. "I don't reckon I do, John. But it would be nice if it happened that way."

Jimbo Fyle came crunching noisily toward them through the snow. Hatch was not with him.

"What're you boys jawin' about here?" Fyle asked merrily. "Don't you know there's a nip in the air? Be more comfortable inside, I'd say."

"As a matter of fact, Mr. Fyle, we were talking about the weather," Waring said. "Not doing anything about it, you understand, but discussing it nonetheless."

"Now you go right ahead an' do somethin' about it if you want, Johnny. Like one

125

of them rainmaker fellas. Say, have you ever seen one of them boys work?" Without waiting for a response he went on. "I seen one out in Californy a few years back, I did. Skinny ol' boy in a beaver high hat an' a claw-hammer coat, he was. A bunch of dirt grubbers hired him an' brung him down from Oregon or some such place.

"Boys, I'll tell you, that old fella come in there with two wagons loaded heavy with big ol' boiling pots and barrels an' barrels of stuff to cook in 'em. Took him the best part of a week to scout out just where he wanted to be an' set all that stuff up to his liking. Hired him a crew of younguns to do his fetching an' carrying and to cut wood an' tend fires.

"Pretty soon he commenced to cooking. Had everybody for fifty mile around gathered there watchin' him. Never did any of that magical sayin' nor dancing nor thumping on drums neither. He just started in to boiling some stuff an' burning other stuff. Awfullest stink there ever was. Steam an' yella smoke in the air, an' him runnin' from fire to fire with little sacks of stuff, throwin' some onto this fire an' putting something else into that pot. He was real worked up about it.

"Boys, he went on like that for three days

an' four nights. There was folks there watchin' 'most all that time an' everybody swore that ole boy couldn't've had himself a wink of sleep the whole while. Anytime night or day whenever you cared to look, there he'd be, runnin' from one place to another, tendin' his pots an' cussing those kids to keep his fires right.

"Fin'ly he give out. Wore hisself plumb out, I guess. Collapsed in a heap by one of them wagons an' didn't wake for the best part of a full day. When he did he sat up, demanded a meal for hisself an' said the job was done. Wanted his pay so he could get on t' the next place.

"Well, them as had hired him said they hadn't seen no rain yet an' wasn't payin' without it. This ol' boy did him some hollering then. Waved a paper at them an' just cussed something fierce, but they wouldn't pay up without they got the rain he'd promised. They packed him up right then an' there and run him off. Told him if he showed his face again in their li'l valley they'd put a stomping on him an' maybe worse. I think they scared the ol' bugger."

Fyle laughed. "I'll tell you somethin' funny that happened just afterward, boys. Inside of two weeks there came up the awfullest storms I ever seen. Rain and lightnin' like you wouldn't b'lieve, and it not stopping. Flooded that whole damn area. Kilt some folks an' ruined others. Washed out th' damn crops those dirt grubbers'd been tryin' to save. Floated off a mess o' houses. Really raised some hell with that valley. An' the funny thing is, there's people who'd still tell you they seen yella smoke an' smelt that awful stink the rainmaker'd made the whole time those storms kept comin' in." He grinned. "Cain't prove none of it by me, you understand, but there's folks out there say they seen it an' smelt it themselves. They're the ones say they should've paid the old boy the way they'd promised to do. Me, I can't say they're wrong neither."

"I've seen water witches," Veach said. "Never saw a rainmaker, but I've known a few diviners that I'd swear could find a well for you. Who's to say the other isn't possible too."

Waring looked amused. "Surely, Veach, you don't believe in these occult sciences and superstitions. Rainmakers? Water witches? Surely not you too."

Veach shrugged. "I just say I don't know, John. Like I told you, I've seen a few diviners at work. And there was water where they said to dig."

"Sheer chance," Waring said, "bolstered by nonsense and flimflammery."

"You wouldn't be doubting *my* word now, would you, Johnny?" Fyle demanded. The cheerfulness had left his tone. It was more warning than question.

"Why would I do that, Mr. Fyle?" Waring responded smoothly. "You said yourself you did not know the cause. I have no reason to doubt you when you say there were floods. That would be demonstrable fact. As to whether your rainmaker caused them, that would be another matter entirely, would it not?"

"I reckon," Fyle grumbled. "Just so you ain't sayin' I lied."

"Of course not," Waring said with an easy smile. "I could see no reason for you to lie about such a thing."

"All right then," Fyle said grumpily. "See if your missus is done in there," he ordered. "It's getting damn cold out here." He turned and walked off.

The other two men watched him out of sight beyond the cabin. Veach turned toward Waring and said, "I notice you told him you didn't find any reason for him to lie about that particular thing, John. You didn't really say if you thought he's a liar. If you don't mind a bit of advice, I'd say you might want

129

to avoid baiting the tiger with Jimbo. That's a game I'd hate to lose with that old boy."

Waring sighed. "I suppose you're right. I wasn't really thinking about it. I suppose I must. For Ann's sake."

"Uh-huh. I really think you should."

"Yes, well . . . I'll go see if she's ready for company."

The man trudged away through the trampled snow, and Veach pulled his gloves off and shoved them into his coat pockets. Despite their protection his fingers felt stiff and were pained by the cold. He reached inside his coat for his cigarette makings, but left them in his pocket when he realized how much trouble he was having trying to distinguish the feel of the paper tag on his tobacco sack drawstring. With so little sense of touch he was certain to waste too much of the flake if he tried to roll a smoke now. He decided to wait until his hands were warm again.

Waring stepped back outside and motioned Veach into the cabin before he walked around the tumble of large boulders in search of Fyle and Hatch.

Veach was more than ready to return to the warmth of the stove within the cabin. In the few minutes that they had been out his hands and his feet both were painfully cold.

He had already lost much of the feeling in his toes. He swiped the back of a hand under his nose and it came away wet, although he had not been able to feel it running. "Helluva day for a picnic," he muttered to himself.

The warmth inside the rock cabin was intensely hot in contrast to the temperature outdoors, even though the fire had not been lighted long enough to bring the heat up to a normally comfortable level. Ann Waring had a blanket wrapped over her shoulders when he went in, but the heat was enough to cause Veach's cheeks and earlobes to tingle.

The woman gave him a wan smile and said, "John tells me it is bad out there this morning."

"Yes, ma'am, but it could be worse. Like Fyle keeps pointing out to us, long as there's no blizzard buildup this stuff will go fast when things start to warm up. And that could happen anytime."

"It would be so much easier if only we could *know.*"

"Oh, I agree for sure, ma'am. But don't worry. Your husband seems a mighty capable man."

She gave him a disturbed look that made it clear that she took no assurance from his

131

opinion. "I . . . suppose so, Mr. Veach. It's just that John hasn't much experience away from the civilized comforts. He's an engineer, not a miner or some mountaineer. It frightens me."

"He's a good man, ma'am. Has a head on his shoulders, I'd say. And sometimes clear thinking is more important than experience. Don't you fret now. He'll take care of you, whatever happens."

Ann Waring shuddered. "Whatever happens. How awful that sounds. And how I wish I knew what that might be." Her voice tailed away.

The door opened with a rush of cold air and the others came inside stamping the snow from their boots. Once all of them were in the cabin it again seemed cramped and even smaller than it was.

CHAPTER 11

Jimbo Fyle stretched, grinning broadly. He stripped his parka off and planted himself in front of the stove, apparently not even noticing that he edged Veach away from the heat when he did so. "By damn, that feels good, boys. Almost better than" — the grin faded into a sly smile and he gave Ann Waring a sideways look that he was careful to let the others see — "well, almost better than anything." The suggestiveness of his thought was boldly displayed, and if he noticed the sudden displeasure on John Waring's face he ignored it.

Fyle turned to face the woman seated on the bunk across the table from him. While he rubbed at his backside he said, "I reckon this would be a good time for you t' fix us a bite of breakfast, little lady. Ol' Jimbo could sure use something in his belly to warm things up an' get the day off to a proper start now. Damn cold out there, it is. An' boil another pot o' that coffee while you're about it, hear? Always like my morning coffee, I do. Don't I, Bo?"

"You do, Jimbo," Hatch agreed seriously. He was perched cross-legged on his rumpled coat and outer clothing beside the door again.

"Yes indeed. I like my comforts of a morning," Jimbo declared firmly.

"You may have to cut back on some of them for a time, Mr. Fyle," Waring said. "I really think we should conserve our supplies now. One light meal a day should be more than enough. And the coffee especially should be saved. It is a stimulant which we might greatly need later."

Fyle glowered at the smaller man. "Are you fixing to go *prudent* on me again, Johnny?" Unexpectedly a grin flashed across his face. "Bet you thought I'd forgot your fancy word, didn't you, Johnny? Well I didn't. Don't you go to downgrading ol' Jimbo, you hear? I ain't so dumb as you think, boy. You'd best be remembering that."

Waring shrugged. "No one implied that you were, Mr. Fyle. But, yes, I do feel that prudence is in order here. We have little enough. We don't dare squander any of it for momentary comfort."

Jimbo snorted out a coarse expletive that

he did not bother to apologize to Ann Waring for. Veach noticed the woman's cheeks flush bright red for a moment. "You wouldn't be tryin' again to be tellin' me what to do, would you, Johnny?"

"What I am trying to do, Fyle, is preserve our supplies for future need," Waring said calmly.

"I think Waring is right," Veach said.

Fyle shifted his attention to Veach and gave him a long, ugly look. "You would," he growled.

Ann Waring came to her feet and stepped around the table to Fyle. "Gentlemen, please! We can all be calm and genteel about this, surely." Using a smile and her fingertips she moved Fyle away from the stove. "Sit down, Mr. Fyle. I can't cook a thing if you are in my way there. John, I am sure I can come up with something hot and filling that will not take too much from our stores." She smiled brightly. "And if I add just the least bit of new coffee to the old grounds I think we can find a solution to that as well. All right?" She shooed a smugly satisfied-looking Jimbo Fyle toward his chair. Veach walked around the table toward his accustomed seat as well. Waring accepted the compromise with good grace, but Veach got the distinct impression that he did not like it.

"Fill the bucket for the little lady," Fyle ordered. He directed the words to no one in particular, but Hatch immediately lumbered to his feet and began pulling his coat on.

"I could do that, Bo Jim," Veach offered. "I guess it's about my turn by now."

"Leave him be," Fyle answered. From all outward indications Hatch might not have heard either of them. He continued to affix the buttons of his coat in place with studied thoroughness.

Bo Jim prepared himself with slow deliberateness, took the bucket and left. Again he tested the door latch several times before his footsteps squeaked faintly away.

"Your partner is an awfully quiet man," Veach offered, simply to make conversation while the woman busied herself at the few sacks that held their supplies.

"I said to leave him be," Fyle snapped. He was clearly annoyed now, glaring at Veach across the small table.

"I was just making talk."

"If you don't have something to say you can keep your damn mouth shut," Fyle told him.

Veach could feel a rise of blood to his face.

His pulse quickened and he could feel his senses grow sharper. Waring stirred uneasily on the bunk behind him.

Ann Waring straightened and turned to touch Fyle lightly on the shoulder. "How would you feel about boiled rice for your breakfast, Mr. Fyle?" she asked. The words were simple enough, but there was an edge of nervousness underlying her tone. She gave him a flickering smile that did not quite ring true.

Veach looked at her closely. She was lovely. As before she reminded him more of an exquisite cameo than of a flesh-and-blood human being. She had fixed her hair while the men were outside and at this early hour it remained perfect, every strand and curl tidily in place, an impeccably fashioned framework for the beauty of her facial features. Her eyes were large and dark and very clear, but troubled now, the steady gaze and total confidence of a few days earlier gone. Her eyes flickered to him and away again. He thought he could read an anxious pleading in her look. Veach swallowed, a taste like bile flooding his throat from the necessity of it, and swallowed away the response he would have liked to fling at Jimbo Fyle.

Large and powerful as Fyle might be, as

intimidatingly commanding as his presence was, in this country he would have to earn his domination, for here a man would allow himself to be pushed only so far. For many the distance was a short one indeed before they would respond with violence. Veach — and Waring as well, he believed — was an ordinary, decent man. Neither of them was of the rough-and-tumble brawling sort that Jimbo Fyle and Bo Jim Hatch seemed to be. But Veach did not want to think of himself as a toady or a milksop either, and pride could shove him into physical confrontation with Fyle or with any other man regardless of the consequences that might be sure to result.

Still, he looked at the anxiety in Ann Waring's eyes and forced his resentment aside. This one time, he thought. For the woman's sake and for that alone.

It bothered him, though, to find within himself a strong sense of relief that he would not have to prove himself by challenging the power that radiated from Jimbo Fyle. He did not dwell upon that knowledge.

Waring sat quietly on the bunk nearby, seemingly unaware of the tension among his wife and his guests. He appeared to be lost in fretful concentration, perhaps on those problems that surrounded the group or on those added concerns that were his alone.

The latch rattled and the door was swung wide. Bo Jim Hatch came in, reached back outside to retrieve the snow-crusted bucket, set it on the floor and carefully closed and latched the door again.

"Thank you, Mr. Hatch," Ann Waring said with a forced lightness. "Would you pour it into this pot, please? Thanks." She gave the huge man a bright smile. Hatch responded with a quick flash of a nervous smile and a dart of his eyes toward Fyle before he turned away. Veach was not sure, but he thought he saw a faint darkening of pleasure-flush on the man's already cold-ruddied cheeks as he turned.

Veach stood and stepped to the front wall of the cabin to claim his coat. He pulled it on and buttoned it.

"You goin' somewhere?" Fyle demanded.

Veach ignored him. He moved behind Fyle to reach for the newly emptied water bucket.

He had scarcely begun to bend when he heard a thin rustle of cloth and almost instantaneously the smooth, oiled *clack* of a revolver hammer being drawn to full cock. Involuntarily he flinched and his motion stopped, leaving him statue-still in a partially bent position with his right hand extended.

Inwardly cursing himself for his reaction, Veach recovered from his surprise. He turned his head to find the muzzle of a short-barreled revolver that had been placed beside his ear. With an odd clarity Veach could see where the drag of metal against leather had rubbed the bluing from either side of the sightless barrel. He could see three light tan bits of lint or leather scrapings caught inside the muzzle itself.

Veach focused his eyes beyond the dark steel of the revolver to Jimbo Fyle's hard and hooded stare. A cold, contemptuous anger began to build deep within Veach, and he took great satisfaction in keeping the emotion out of his expression and his voice.

"I take it you object to me using this bucket," he said. His voice was steady if somewhat strained. He did not mind the strain as long as he could avoid any fear-quaver there.

Fyle's face had been set, blank and unreadable as the rock walls of the cabin. Now he tilted his head back and grinned. He eased the hammer down and put the revolver away. "Coulda been a hell of a joke on you, couldn't it, boy?" he said with real amusement.

"Yeah, Jimbo. *Real* funny."

"Ah, don't take it personal now," Fyle said with good humor. "No harm done, was there? You just kinda startled me there. Thought you was gonna bean me or something, see. Now me, I'm a gentle kind of fella myself. Never go lookin' for trouble. But you never know about folks, so sometimes you just gotta be kinda careful, see. You might remember that, boy. Jus' be kinda careful." He grinned broadly again. "I'd sure *hell* hate to shoot somebody by *accident.*"

Veach ignored the emphasis the man placed on the word accident. The meaning was clear enough. He continued his delayed reach for the water bucket and straightened with it.

CHAPTER 12

Veach stamped his feet on the ice-crusted rocks lining the thin trickle of the creek flow, greatly reduced now except for a swift-running stream center, and cursed his own sloppiness in getting his glove wet. What should have been a minor annoyance now became a major torment. Unwilling for the woman's sake to express his anger with Fyle and unwilling for his own self-image to vent his unhappiness with himself for feeling a gut-wrenching surge of fear when he looked down the barrel of Jimbo Fyle's revolver, Veach was on safer ground with the wet glove. He let the rage find expression now, cursing softly but bitterly into the white-and-black silence of the frozen gorge floor.

He felt the oddly burnlike sensation in his fingers where the water gave access to the cold through the damp glove. He cursed again and then, at least partially relieved of the burden of unexpressed frustration, he was able to laugh at himself for doing so. He dipped the bucket full in the creek and made his way awkwardly back toward the cabin. He struggled to carry the burden back with his right arm held stiffly and uncomfortably away from his body. If any of the cold water slopped over the edge he wanted it on the ground and not down his trouser leg.

"What's that for?" Fyle wanted to know when Veach was back inside and stripping his coat and wet gloves off.

Veach took time to inspect the rice pot before he answered. Ann Waring's water was hot, but not yet boiling. The stove heat felt good to him. "I thought I'd shave after breakfast, if Mrs. Waring will let me warm some water here. Might do us all some good, as a matter of fact."

Fyle fingered his stubble, much heavier than Veach's, and grunted.

"I believe we would feel better if we clean up a little," Waring agreed. "I have a decent razor if anyone needs to borrow one." He added drily, "And I believe we can find a mirror." Veach remembered the collection of combs and curlers and mirrors Ann Waring had had out when he arrived. Mirrors would be no problem here.

"Well now, Johnny, maybe we'll just scrape

down at that," Fyle said. "Get all prettied up. Sure, it might be puttin' all of us in a better mood. Your friend here could use that most 'specially." He hooked a thumb toward Veach.

"Meaning what, mister?" Veach snapped.

"You jus' seem a little touchy this morning, boy. That's all. My oh my, boy. You an' me do seem to be gettin' crossways of one another today. See what I mean?" Jimbo Fyle tilted his head back and laughed as if he had just told a fine joke. He dropped his hand and scratched himself contentedly.

"I, for one, think it would be a fine idea for you gentlemen to shave and wash. You in particular, John," the woman said lightly. "In the meantime you can wash your hands. Breakfast will be ready in a few minutes."

The rice, when it came, was glued into sticky clumps by unwashed starch from the grains. Veach found boiled rice barely palatable at best. Ann Waring's version was even worse than usual, but neither he nor any of the others offered complaint. They sat in silence and spooned up the tasteless but hot and belly-filling food. Their jaws worked with the mechanical thoroughness of a steam-driven engine and with much the same enthusiasm. The coffee was better. It was pale and weakly brewed, but at least was close to what they wanted. The aroma from the steaming mugs alone was almost enough to satisfy.

"Damn good, little lady," Fyle said when he was finished. "Me an' Bo Jim do thank you. 'Deed we do."

"Not at all, Mr. Fyle." Her words were offhandedly casual, but she seemed genuinely pleased by the compliment. She began collecting and washing the few bowls and spoons they had used. "Shall I put your shaving water on the stove?"

"Why that'd be real nice, little lady. Just real nice of you." Fyle apparently had appropriated the idea as his own.

Veach dug into his war bag for his old razor. From one of the trunks piled in the corner at the foot of the bunk Waring produced a flat case holding a pair of matched and balanced razors of a quality few barbers might own. They drew a thin whistle of appreciation from Veach.

Waring smiled. "A gift from my father several years ago. You're welcome to use one if you wish," he offered.

"I'd like to do that, John." He gave his own stained blade a rueful glance. "I hope you have soap to go with those. I'm out."

"A little. Not much. Mr. Fyle?"

"Huh?"

145

"Would you and Mr. Hatch have a cake of soap with you?"

"Hell, Johnny, me an' Bo don't even own a razor. Just borry one sometimes. We'll jus' wet an' scrape anyhow though." He reached forward without invitation and took Veach's razor from the table. "This thing's good enough for us." He laughed. "Jimbo an' Bo Jim don't hafta be fancy about things."

Ann Waring set a pot of warm water on the table and the men shaved, Fyle hurrying through an indifferent job of it without bothering to strop the borrowed razor. Bo Jim Hatch, however, approaching the table only after Fyle was finished, was thoroughly absorbed in the task of finding and eliminating the last hair from his beard. When he was finally done his face was pink-cheeked and smooth.

"Why, Mr. Hatch," Ann Waring said. "Excuse me for being personal, please, but you look so nice now. Really you do."

The change was remarkable. Clean-shaven and with his hair finger-brushed back away from his forehead, Bo Jim Hatch was not a bad-looking man, huge in size but all bone and muscle, slightly flat facial features now dominated and made almost attractive by the strikingly pale eyes with pinpoint black pupils. The effect of his eyes gave him the same near-savage fascination as that drawn to a captive and half-tamed wolf. If Hatch's face had been molded by an underlying animation and intelligence instead of slack disinterest, he would have been handsome.

At the woman's words Bo Jim Hatch shifted his attention to her, staring at her long and hard as if he were trying to absorb into memory every feature of form and face. It was the first time he had given any outward attention to her or to any of the others in the cabin save Jimbo Fyle. He gave Ann Waring a slow, spreading smile, and the illusion of handsomeness vanished. Coming from any other man such a look would have been rawly suggestive. On Hatch it was suggestive yet somehow remote.

"Sit down, Bo," Fyle ordered.

Hatch's expression faded to a blank again and then struggled back toward puzzlement. "The lady likes me, Jimbo," he said.

"You're a good boy, Bo. Everybody knows that. Now go set down."

"Sure, Jimbo." Hatch turned away and resumed his cross-legged seat by the door, but now his attention was on Ann Waring. His eyes followed her every motion as she threw out the used shaving water and cleaned up after the men.

"I told you not to pay any mind to the

little lady, didn't I, Bo Jim? Didn't I tell you that?"

"I guess you did, Jimbo."

"Well quit your staring then. I tol' you to mind your manners. Now do it."

"I will, Jimbo." His eyes no longer followed the woman, but there was a decided cant of his head toward her and it was obvious that his attention remained on her whereabouts. After a moment he lumbered to his feet and said, "I'll bring more water in, Jimbo, ready for the next use, all right?" It was the first time Hatch had volunteered himself for anything. Except for his pleading that Fyle tell about their fight, it was the first conversation he had initiated. It might have been a gift of sorts, an offering to Ann Waring of a service he could perform for her instead of for Jimbo.

"Not now, Bo Jim. I'll tell you when." Fyle's tone was crisp.

"All right, Jimbo." Hatch subsided, withdrew back into himself, but for a brief instant Veach thought he saw a hint of resentment flash through Bo Jim Hatch's pale eyes.

The prospect of a clash between Hatch and Jimbo Fyle disturbed him. However unlikely it might be, the merest possibility was distressing in their confined situation.

Veach had heard too many ugly stories about the tensions and the angers that could develop among people in close and isolated confinement. Cabin fever they called it here. Even if the stories were wildly exaggerated he did not want to see an example of a fever like that in actual practice — especially since a battle between titans might place himself and the Warings, perhaps particularly Ann Waring, at the center of the maelstrom. And a conflict between Jimbo Fyle and Bo Jim Hatch would most certainly be a battle of titans. Veach hoped such a thing would not arise. He was sure from the guarded look on the man's face that John Waring had noticed the same thing, and likely would be having similar worries now.

Of them all, only Ann Waring seemed unaware of the impact her casually offered comment had had. When she finished tidying the cabin she rearranged her mirrors on the small table.

"Mr. Veach, would you mind moving over beside John? If you gentlemen are going to be so neat and nice-looking today I really should do something with my appearance too." She smiled prettily and arched her eyebrows.

Veach had no choice but to comply, although he thought it a poor time for her to be making herself even prettier. Yet he knew there was nothing her husband could say openly to dissuade her without making an issue of it and probably making it only worse. He left the table and moved over to perch on the side rail of the bunk beside Waring.

The woman gathered her combs and brushes from the polished leather traveling case full of such gear and placed a set of curling irons on the stove. She sat at the table and arranged everything to her liking before she began to unpin her hair.

The pale silvery-gold hair tumbled free in a shimmering cascade that caught and held the lamplight from above. Between the waterfall glory of that hair and the way her upraised arms pulled the bodice of her dress against firm, delicately tipped breasts, she was a sight of extraordinary loveliness. And desirability.

She took one of the shell-backed brushes and began to pull it slowly through her hair. To no one in particular she said, "My hair is just *so* awful. A hundred strokes a day are needed just to keep it *bearable.*" She did not sound nearly so aggrieved as her words might have indicated.

The rise and fall of her arms and the changing light patterns in her hair as the brush bristles smoothed and pulled at it were inexpressibly sensuous. Veach knew the most polite thing to do would have been to look away, to enter into a conversation with Waring. He did not. He wanted instead to take the brush from her and perform the task himself. The pads of his fingers felt smooth and silken as he imagined the feel of that hair under them. He began to blush.

The woman silently mouthed her counting of the strokes, turning her head to meet the pull of the brush as languorously as a cat allowing itself to be stroked by a favored human.

After a moment John Waring stood and moved behind her. He took the brush from her fingers and stroked her hair with the back of his hand. With a tight smile directed not to but certainly for the other men in the cabin he said, "Let me finish that, dear." With a hollow, jealous stab in his belly Veach realized that the man was affirming his claim to this woman.

She twisted her head to smile up at her husband with open delight, and Veach wondered if she was aware of this interplay, if she might be enjoying receiving the admiration of her husband and these strangers. "How thoughtful of you, John. I've counted twenty-three strokes so far."

Veach wrenched his head away from the sight of her and wished he could direct his thoughts as easily. Jimbo Fyle and Bo Jim Hatch were engrossed in the scene, and Veach wondered if their restraint was any better than his own. Or as good. For Waring's sake he hoped so. Because his own was being taxed.

CHAPTER 13

Fyle left his chair about an hour later to tug open the stove door and cram more lengths of split wood into the firebox. Waring watched with apparent displeasure. Fyle was refueling the stove heavily and often.

"We really don't need to burn that much wood," Waring cautioned.

"Ah hell, Johnny, I'll get ol' Bo Jim to fetch in some more. There's plenty piled out there an' more to be cut if we need. No sense bein' cold atop of everything else."

"I wasn't thinking of inconvenience, Fyle. I just feel we should conserve the wood as well as our food."

Fyle gave him a derisive laugh. "Johnny, you worry more'n any fella I ever seen before. Damned if you don't. You got wood enough there t'last for weeks. Damned old maid is what you are about all this. You jus' trust ol' Jimbo an' you needn't fret so much."

"I know we have several weeks' supply of fuel," Waring explained patiently. "It is what comes afterward that I have the foresight to think about now, even if you do not."

"You can just watch your mouth there, Johnny. I don't take so good to folks talkin' to me like that." There was harsh warning in his voice. "Bo Jim! Carry in another boxful of wood."

Hatch climbed to his feet and laboriously began to button himself into his coat. "Can I bring in the lady's water now, Jimbo?"

"Huh?"

"Can I . . ."

"Oh. Yeah. You do that, Bo Jim. Bring the water too. Maybe the little lady'll boil those coffee grounds again, eh?"

Bo Jim bobbed his head and went toward the water bucket. Fyle stopped him with a hard look and an outthrust arm. "What was it I told you t' do, Bo Jim?" he demanded.

"You said I should fetch in water and wood, Jimbo," Hatch answered.

"No, dammit. I told you t' get the wood in, and that's what I want done first. Better yet, I want you to step around first an' see is there anything out there that needs some shooting. *Then* you can bring in the wood. *Then* you can fetch your damned water."

"All right, Jimbo."

154

When Hatch was outside Jimbo Fyle shook his head in disgust. "Sorry 'bout that, folks, but I swear I do get annoyed with that boy from time to time. Good hearted a ol' boy as there ever was, do anything I tell him to regardless, but I swear does that boy once get an idea in his head he won't ever turn loose of it 'til he's done whatever he set out after or I pull him off of it. An' even then sometimes I've had to slap him around some to make him quit a thing."

Jimbo shook his head again and checked the coffeepot. It was empty. "He'll have the water in directly," he muttered. To the others he said, "I'll tell you one about that ol' boy. There was a time when we was down in the Breaks. Might've been in the Indian Nations then or maybe Texas or New Mexico. They kinda run together there, so I ain't real sure. Rough country, anyhow. Anyway we was on horses that'd been used pretty hard an' we decided to lay up for a few days an' let them rest. Do us a little loafing and take things easy by a little pothole o' water we found there.

"We set up a little ways off from the water an' that next morning we seen some free-running horses come in for a drink. Good-looking animals, too. They hadn't been mustanged out. Not this bunch. Clean-limbed,

155

tough-looking herd, they was. An' in with them was a young stud that was just the spit, I mean the very picture of the Pacing White Stallion. I s'pose you know about him."

Veach nodded, but both of the Warings shook their heads in puzzlement.

"You never heard of the Pacin' White Stallion? Sure did think everybody west of St. Louis would've heard about him, b'damn. Sure did. Now I don't put no stock in it myself, you understand, but 'most anybody has a story t' tell about the Pacing White Stallion." Fyle shook his head in wonder at the Warings' lack of knowledge.

"You can hear him called by a dozen different names, but the horse is 'most always the same. Big an' wild an' free-runnin' studhorse, you see. White horse. Long mane and tail an' so pretty he'd take a man's breath away. Mostly they say he's a pacer. But they *all* say there never was a faster horse nor one that could last half so long atraveling. There's people will tell you they've run him themselves, seen him and run him day an' night with relays of horses for the chase, run him better'n three hundred mile and him outlast every man an' every horse they had. Never been caught, they say, nor never will be.

156

"Like I said, I don't believe all that stuff myself, though there's folks as does. All I say is that this here young studhorse looked like the Pacing White Stallion is *supposed* to look, which naturally got our attention on him, you see. No way it wouldn't after all the stories you hear.

"Anyway, me an' Bo Jim was laid up in camp there and got a look at this horse, an' we just as naturally got to talkin' about them stories an' people tryin' to catch the Pacing White Stallion an' how they all said they'd tried to do it.

"Well I went an' mentioned how I'd heard it said that back east th' Indians used to walk down deer an' such game for food and that if a man really had the guts — 'scuse me, little lady — he could walk down a horse too, just by stayin' after it, not hurrying or running, mind, but just walking after it 'till he wore it plumb down an' could walk up close enough to put a rope on it.

"Now that ain't something I claim to've ever done my own self, you understand. It's just something I've heard told. I never claimed no different." Jimbo leaned back and tucked his thumbs into his belt.

"Wouldn't you know, though, th' next morning ol' Bo Jim was already up an' gone when I tossed my blankets off. Left his horse where it was, an' his saddle, but he'd carried his rope with him. Well I knowed where he'd gone, sure as if he'd come out an' said it. That ol' boy was gonna walk down a white horse. Though what in hell he would want with a white horse I never could figure.

"I piled more chips on the fire an' set the coffee on to boil an' snuck a look off toward the waterhole an' sure enough, here come those horses mousing up toward it with a ugly old mare a-leading them. Before they ever got to the water out come ol' Bo Jim at a walk, him whistling an' with a rope hung over his shoulder.

"Well them wild horses was shy but they didn't exactly spook, you see. They just kinda backed off an' turned away from that particular hole without gettin' too excited about it. Far as they could see, I guess, they wasn't bein' chased by this fella out for a morning walk. So they turned away an' Bo Jim just walked on behind them. We was camped up on kind of a higher place where you could see real good most directions, so I sat an' watched for a spell. After a time them horses got to feeling a little crowded so they took off into a lope an' left ol' Bo Jim way back in the dust. Pretty soon you couldn't see no horses anymore, but Bo Jim was still steppin' along in their tracks. A few hours more an' you couldn't even see that much.

"He never come in at all that night. Next morning, there was the wild bunch, gettin' their regular drink at the waterhole. If they was being bothered by Bo Jim tryin' to walk them down they sure wasn't showing it much. They got their drink and went off about their business. Coupla hours later here comes Bo Jim, still carryin' that rope an' about as wore down and drug out as ever a man could be, you'd think. Looked like hell, he did. Covered with dust an' sweat an' limping pretty bad from all that walking in boots meant for ridin' horseback instead of chasing horses afoot.

"Well I sat for the longest time an' watched him come. Figured he'd have himself a drink an' climb on up to the camp for a bite to eat an' some sleep. But I reckon I didn't know him as good then as I do now, for he went to the water just like I'd figured but he never even looked up toward the camp. Just got a good drink an' bowed his neck and went off after them horses again. He was still in sight into the afternoon, so he'd slowed down considerable from the way he'd been going the day before.

"He wasn't stopped, though. Not by a

damn sight he wasn't. Next day it was the same thing. The horses drifted in for their drink, easy as could be, the white stud among them, an' Bo Jim following behind but later'n ever. Late morning it was before he got to the water. Well this time I was *sure* he'd be comin' up to camp. Damned fool never did. Got his drink an' went right on walking, except now he was hobbling like some sort of crip. You never seen a man hippety-hop so bad as he done.

"Well now, I watched him a spell an' decided I'd best take a hand in it, so I threw his saddle on his old horse, which was rested pretty good by then, an' got on my own an' went down to collect him. Damn fool never paid me no mind at all. Wouldn't get on that horse. Never said a word. Just kept walkin'. An' I hadn't carried any food with me, thinking to take him back to camp, you see. Far as I knew he hadn't stopped to eat nor anything in two days. Wouldn't stop then neither. So I went back to camp and got a little sack o' food and carried it back to him. He took that all right. Ate it while he walked. After a spell I said the hell with him an' went back.

"Next morning the horses come in as usual an' Bo Jim not far behind them. He'd taken a shortcut on them, you see, though he still wasn't anywheres close to them. I don't figure they so much as knew he was back there. He was walking a little better then. Turned out he'd sliced the sides of his boots so they wouldn't bind so where his feet was swole up inside them. I carried food down to him again an' he kept a-walkin'.

"Next day he was *still* movin', but barely. He was way behind the horses again, short-cut or no. An' I was fixing to run out of food myself. So this time I carried his horse down an' told him to crawl on, we was riding north and to hell with them wild horses, white stallion or no white stallion.

"Ol' Bo, he never answered me, so I clumb down off my horse an' gave Bo a thump, just a tap really, that dropped him face down in that little pothole o' water. Reckon he'd have drownded if I hadn't hauled him outta there. Threw him across his saddle and dragged him back up to camp.

"That old boy slept straight through to the next morning an' woke up mad. Soon as his head come up off the saddle he opened his mouth an' said, 'Jimbo, you tol' me a man can walk a horse down, didn't you?'

"I said, 'No, Bo Jim, I tol' you that there's some folks as say a man could walk a horse down. I never claimed that myself.'

"Bo Jim, he gave me a long, real quiet look an' fin'ly he said, 'Damn!' 'Scuse me, little lady, but that's just what he said. An' that's the *last* thing he ever said about tryin' to walk down the Pacing White Stallion. Never even mentioned it when he had t' buy a new pair o' boots in place of the good ones he'd gone and ruined, and I haven't heard him mention none of it since. Nor I don't talk about it much myself when Bo Jim's around. He's a notional kind of ol' boy, an' you never know what he might go an' do. But I'll tell you this . . . I believe that boy woulda kept walkin' after that fool horse 'til one of them dropped. An' I don't reckon it would've been the horse to drop first."

Fyle sat back and gave them a firm nod of his head. Ann Waring laughed and asked for — and received — more stories about the Pacing White Stallion while Veach and John Waring made another inroad on Veach's dwindling tobacco supply. They were talking about the legendary horse when Hatch returned with a huge armload of wood, but if he made any connection between their talk and his own past experience he gave no indication of it. He put the stove-lengths into Waring's woodbox, picked up the bucket and left again.

The oddest thing about all of it, Veach decided, was not the story, but the fact that Veach believed it. He was quite thoroughly satisfied that Jimbo Fyle had told the absolute and literal truth about it. And that made it more awesome than amusing. Veach was barely able to repress a shudder. Bo Jim Hatch frightened him, he realized, in a way no other man ever had.

CHAPTER 14

By midafternoon Jimbo Fyle was showing signs of nervousness. He began scratching under his freshly shaven chin and soon had the skin there abraded and reddened. He stood and stretched, his knuckles easily coming into contact with the mud-covered poles supporting the roof. When he stretched it seemed that the walls of the cabin must surely tumble outward, unable to contain him. He stamped his boots a few times to loosen his leg muscles and stalked the length of the narrow opening between table and stove.

"You said you didn't have cards, huh, Johnny?"

"No. Sorry. Nor dice or other amusements," Waring said.

Fyle cursed aloud. He cocked his head and directed a narrowed eye toward Ann Waring. "Guess you didn't need none at that," he said.

Waring flushed red with a sudden rush of blood to his head, but his expression did not change. His eyes did not narrow. If anything they softened slightly as if with a quiet amusement.

It was Veach who openly responded to the comment. "See here now, Fyle, there's no need for that kind of talk."

Fyle stopped his pacing and leaned across the table toward Veach. "You've been prodding at me all day, boy. I don't know how you figure any of this is your never-mind, but you can keep your mouth shut. Open it again an' I may throw your butt outta here. Let you cool off outside tonight, boy. How's that sound?"

Veach paled, but he would not back down now. Eyes locked on Fyle's, he started to rise. His belly suddenly felt tightly knotted and empty in a way that had nothing to do with food. He grinned at the bulkier man and said, "I might come cheap, Jimbo, but I don't come free for nothing."

Fyle straightened and took a quick side-step that placed him closer to Bo Jim Hatch. "Cheap enough."

Bo Jim's attention had come awake from whatever distant place it rested in while he was seated and waiting, and Waring was licking his lips, preparing himself to come off the bunk and join in when it became necessary.

Ann Waring yelped, the noise sharp and ringing inside the close stone walls. She leaped forward, a strand of her re-pinned hair coming undone and bouncing down over her right eye. She placed herself between them with her back to Jimbo Fyle. With both hands she shoved Veach's chest, pushing him back toward his chair. "Stop it!" Her voice was shrill, close to panic in her fright.

Shaken and trembling though she was, there was an unexpected strength in her slender wrists and long, slim fingers. Veach yielded to her urgency and allowed himself to be pushed back down. "Please. Please, Mr. Veach."

She whirled to face Jimbo Fyle. Her voice was quavering, unsteady. "Mr. Fyle. Sit down." She pointed toward the other chair, and in spite of her agitation there was a brisk crackle of command in her tone. "I will *not* have this in my house," she declared. Angrily she marched toward the burly Fyle. Her fists were clenched and her jaw outthrust. Anger flared in her eyes. "I said sit *down,* sir." One long finger pointed demandingly toward the empty chair. "Now *do* it." She advanced on him another step until she was positioned defiantly beneath his chin, her head tilted back. She was breathing heavily in short, rapid gasps.

Jimbo Fyle turned and after a moment let out his breath. As the tension left his muscles he seemed to deflate to a slightly smaller size. He barked out a short, choppy laugh and gave the woman an insolent grin that twisted the left corner of his mouth. "My oh my, little lady," he said, "ol' Jimbo will do jus' like you say. Umm-mmm! 'Deed I will." He laughed again and swooped lightly into the chair. "You c'n calm down now, little lady. Sure wouldn't wanta do nothing to upset you. No indeed." He laughed lightly. There was no hint of belligerance in his voice or manner now.

Ann Waring looked confused. She turned again toward Veach. "You!" she said accusingly. "I will thank you, sir, to keep your comments to yourself. Do you understand me?"

He did not, for he had only been trying to defend her, but he gave her a shrug that could have been interpreted as agreement.

John Waring was beside her, although she had not seen him stand and move to her. He took her elbow and gently guided her back to their bunk. "It's all right now, dear." In a voice pitched so that the others could plainly hear he said, "It will be all right now. You did just fine. Nothing to worry about now. You see, we're all bored. And a little apprehensive. A flare of temper was to be expected, you see." Waring shifted his eyes toward Fyle and then Veach. Still pretending to direct his words toward his wife he said, "We all will have to be careful in the future to avoid irritating others. Do you see that?"

She sat primly and gave him a firm nod of her head. She seemed somewhat proud of herself now. "I do, John." Looking levelly at Veach and at Fyle she added, "See that you gentlemen do too."

Veach returned a short, reassuring nod. Jimbo Fyle grinned at her.

She hid her hands in a fold of her skirt on her lap. Her fingers were trembling, but her agitation had the appearance of exhilaration rather than fear or anger. She was a gently raised woman, Veach reminded himself. This might well have been the first time she had ever really exerted her influence as a woman — as a person — over people outside her own close circle of family and friends.

"It must be about time to bring those animals in for the night," Veach said.

"Fine." The prospect of fresh air and

physical activity was bound to be attractive. The interior of the cabin was beginning to feel — and to smell — too closely confining. Waring took his coat from the wall peg and handed Veach his.

" 'Bout time for some supper too, ain't it? An' you boys leave me an' Bo Jim's horses alone. Don't go running them around," Fyle complained. He hooked his thumbs in his belt and leaned back to watch darkly while Waring and Veach pulled their coats on. "Well?" he demanded.

"What?" Waring asked.

"Are you gonna tell your woman to cook or ain't you?"

"Mr. Fyle, I don't *tell* my wife to perform her duties. When we return I will look at what we have left and will ask her to do what I think best." He emphasized the word "ask."

That emphasis seemed to please Ann Waring. It could be taken as a sign of new respect for her in the wake of her assertiveness a few hours earlier. She accepted it as an earned compliment and smiled primly. Jimbo Fyle scowled.

Veach and Waring finished their preparation to face the cold outside. As Waring reached for the door latch Fyle said, "Don't forget about those animals of mine."

"I have no intention of disturbing your livestock, Mr. Fyle," Waring responded patiently.

Fyle grunted his approval.

The weather was unchanged, the sky a clear and brilliant blue, the air crackling with a deep and silent cold. The snow underfoot squeaked shrilly. The sun was long since out of sight behind intervening rock, and the remaining light had a pale and watery quality despite the clarity of the air.

"I wonder where the temperature sits right now," Veach mused while he rubbed the back of a gloved hand under his nose.

Waring raised his head and flared his nostrils as if he could gauge the temperature that way. "Not too bad," he judged. "Fifteen below. No more than twenty, anyway, I'd say."

"No sign of change, either." Veach searched the sky, but found not the first hazy forerunner of incoming cloud cover. "It will be plain damned cold before morning."

Waring smiled. "If I had a boy now, why tomorrow morning might be a good time to get him to taste a tire iron. If I had a wagon."

Veach laughed. He too as a child had been told about the delightfully sweet taste of frozen iron, and on a morning much like the morrow should bring. His father and older brother had left him tongue-frozen and firmly attached to the wheel of a grain drill for five interminably long minutes until they brought a bucket of water to sluice over the wheel — and the boy — and free him from the trap. Two years later he had done as much for his sister and had gotten a strapping for his efforts, that and a lecture on the difference between boys and girls and how they should be treated. Veach smiled and thought that if he ever had a son of his own he would have to remember to teach him both of those lessons.

Waring chuckled as if he had been having similar thoughts. Aloud he said, "Wouldn't you know they'd have wandered clear to the next drift."

The horses and mules were bunched far downstream and on the far side of the gorge floor. "Yeah, wouldn't you," Veach agreed. He was not at all displeased about having to walk a little farther to collect the animals.

The men set out through the loose and now exceptionally dry snow toward the animals. They walked without hurry in companionable silence, dividing their paths by unspoken agreement as they neared the mules. Veach split his roan gelding away from the other horses and hazed him toward the mules. At a comfortable walking pace they drove the horse and the three leggy mules up the gorge to Waring's shelter.

"It's a shame there isn't more for them to forage on," Veach said as he slid the last barrier pole into place across the shed opening.

"Nothing to be done about it now, I'm afraid."

"No. Nothing." The roan had been in poor flesh to begin with and looked even worse now. Its patchy, incomplete winter coat made it look all the poorer, positively ragged to the eye, although it was the gauntness beneath that hair that now disturbed Veach. He would be able to ask little from this horse when they were ready to leave. Simple transportation — if that — would be the extent of its usefulness. Bucking drifted snow would be far beyond its weakened abilities. The mules were in far better condition, still sleek and strong.

Waring seemed to catch Veach's train of thought. "When we go out," he said, "we'll want to travel together at least to Joe Huntingdon's place. He should have some barn-fed horses there. If you wish, it might be better when we leave for Ann to ride your animal. We can use the mules to break trail, and she can follow on your gelding."

"That's mighty good of you, John."

"Not really. Just simple cooperation. Something we all may need to do a great deal of."

"Yeah." Veach directed an unfocused gaze down the gorge toward and beyond the horses that were still pawing into the snow there. "But I think some of us are willing to cooperate more than others."

"Patience, Mr. Veach. I am told it is a virtue."

"I'm not long on all the virtues, John."

Waring grinned suddenly, a bright and flashing look that bespoke an eagerness that was contained but not nonexistent. "Nor am I always, Mr. Veach, although I do try. I do try."

Veach felt somehow reassured by the few words spoken. He smiled and said, "Let's go see what good ol' Jimbo is having for his supper."

Waring smiled. "I might object more if I weren't so hungry myself."

Veach rubbed his own flat and hollow-feeling stomach in agreement. They turned and squeaked their way back toward the cabin.

Chapter 15

"Johnny-boy, you'd best teach this wo—"
Fyle tried to say as they entered the cabin.

"Hush!" Her voice was sharp. She
sounded certain now of her right to direct
the actions and the statements of those
around her. "I told you to be quiet, Mr.
Fyle. I expect you to do so." She turned to
face her husband. Waring was still in his
coat and snow-crusted boots.

Waring had come in still in a good humor
from the memories brought out by his talk
with Veach. He smiled indulgently and immediately the woman bridled, although Waring seemed not to notice the subtle changes
in the set of her features. "Are you having
some difficulty, dear?" he asked mildly.

She tossed her head. "Would you care?"
she snapped back at him.

Looking hurt and puzzled, Waring recoiled
from the retort. "Why . . . of course. Whatever would make you think otherwise?"

"Well, you certainly don't show any concern for me any more. You could at least take me seriously when I approach you with a problem. Or is that too much to ask?" There was no mistaking her annoyance now.

Waring stammered out an apology that she did not listen to. Instead she half turned toward Fyle and thrust a finger toward him. "I will *not*," she declared, "be ordered about by this man. Do you understand that, John? I won't have it. I simply will not have it. I expect you to make that clear, and if you will not then I shall do it myself." Her eyes were flashing darkly.

John Waring rubbed the back of his neck and said, "I believe you have already done so, dear. You can consider it an accomplished fact."

Fyle seemed not at all upset by her outburst, in fact gave every indication of being amused by it. A half-hidden smile twisted the corners of his mouth and there was a new level of interest in the way he eyed the woman. He planted his hands on his hips and grinned at her. He ignored Waring and Veach.

"What is this all about, anyway?" Waring asked.

His wife glared at him as if she expected him to know. Fyle tilted his head back and laughed. "Not hardly a damn thing, Johnny," he said. "Sure is funny the way a woman'll get notional, though, when you tell 'em the least little thing to do. Sure is. This one now, Johnny. You oughta teach her some manners, see? Does a man say jump a woman oughta be in the air 'fore she takes time to ask how high."

Ann Waring's cheeks colored a bright red with renewed anger. She gave her husband an accusatory stare, as if it were his fault that Fyle felt that way. And that the man said so. She stamped the few paces to the edge of their bed and flounced into a coldly withdrawn seat on the most distant edge of the bunk.

"I still don't know what either of you is talking about," Waring said uncertainly.

Fyle chuckled. He seemed to be enjoying himself. "Ah, Johnny, I jus' told her to do some cooking, see, you bein' out fooling with them mules or you woulda done it yourself, see, an' she got her hackles raised just for that. Cute as a damn painter cat cub, too, an' feisty as a lynx, I swear." He laughed in her direction — she was pointedly ignoring him — and said, "I kinda like that, little lady. Damn me if I don't."

"It sounds like a simple matter of misunderstanding," Waring said carefully. "Ann, I am sure Mr. Fyle meant no harm in making his request. His ways are simply . . . different from ours. And Mr. Fyle, my wife's point is that you have no right to instruct her, nor to demand services from her. As indeed you do not. If you will remember that in the future I am sure we will have no more discord." He smiled politely at each of them.

Behind Waring Bo Jim Hatch's attention swung from the vacant distance of his patient waiting to concentrate on the back of John Waring's neck. Veach, standing forgotten by the coat pegs, noticed the sudden focus of Hatch's interest when Waring spoke to correct Jimbo Fyle. The cold intensity of Hatch's gaze sent a shiver up the length of Veach's spine.

"Meant no harm," Ann Waring mocked without looking at her husband. "Well, aren't we the mealymouthed one now." She snapped her head around to send another glare knifing in his direction. "I'll tell you this, John Waring. You and your friends can do your own cooking tonight. You won't get *me* to wait on you hand and foot like some common servingwoman."

Waring's sigh was lost under the sound of thunderous laughter from Jimbo Fyle. Fyle's laughter did nothing, though, to reduce the intensity of the attention Waring was getting from Bo Jim Hatch.

Veach stepped forward and edged around Fyle to get to the stove. Without speaking he added wood to the fire and began piling the too-light sacks holding their supplies onto the work shelf beside the stove. Behind him Fyle grinned and John Waring sat gingerly on the side of the bunk, but as far from his wife as he could manage without being conspicuous about it. As soon as he was seated Hatch's attention lapsed again into a vacancy of expression.

Fyle sat also, seemingly as content to be waited on by Veach as by the woman, and within minutes was again chattering to the room at large, this time about a teamster he said he had once known, a man who Fyle alleged could balance the gaits and the pull of a ten-up of mules with no controls other than his own cursing. "Never used even a jerkline, ol' Harry didn't," Fyle asserted, "nor never needed one. He'd been with them mules three years an' they knew better'n to cross him." To judge from Jimbo Fyle's light and idle tone the man might never have known a moment of friction in his lifetime, far less a few minutes ago.

Veach took the stack of bowls down from the shelf where they were stored and distributed them on the small table. "You know something about freighters then, Fyle?" he asked.

"Ah now, I know a little somethin' about most everything," Fyle declared easily. "An' I reckon you do too, huh?"

"Not about everything," Veach said with a smile, "but about freighters I do, yes."

"You've driven, then?"

Veach laughed. "Not unless I have to. Which happens from time to time when a driver is, uh, taken under the weather, so to speak. But I'm just barely good enough for a fill-in, and I know it. That's a job that takes an expert on the lines."

"Ayup. For sure." Despite a casualness of tone Fyle's eyes narrowed slightly in interest. "An' just what is it you do that you'd be fillin' in for the experts?"

"Oh, I'm in the stay-at-home end of the business. Terminal agent, you see. All the dull paperwork and the scheduling. Pay the bills and see that the livestock stays healthy. Fret a lot about whether the drivers and the wipers will show up on time. Things like that."

"An agent, huh? Why you could be a good fella t' know then if a man wanted to be doin' some shipping. Where is it you'd be doin' all this?" Fyle asked, openly interested now.

Veach looked at the tightly closed door with a rueful grin. "*If* I get there in time that Whacker doesn't give the job to some-body else, I'll be taking over an end-of-run terminal over in the Idaho country for Whacker Stevens. He's opened a new line over there. Going into business for himself and hauling into some of the new camps over there. We worked together in Montana, and he asked me to come over and give him a hand. I figured I might as well do it."

"Stevens, huh?" Jimbo mused. He shook his head. "Nope. Don't know him nor any Stevens Express, but I reckon I will. I kinda like to keep up with who's haulin' what and to where. You could say it's like a hobby with me, see. Such things interest me. What'll you be haulin' over there?"

Veach felt himself warming toward Fyle, at least a little. It had been some time since he had had an opportunity to discuss his work. And most people seemed to find it rather dull in comparison with the big-strike potential that lured the miners to the camps their wagons served or with the independent spirit and the uncertainties of road dangers that faced the drivers on the stage and freight lines. Practically no one wanted to listen to a terminal agent discuss his job. They were always much more interested in stories the drivers could tell about dangerous fords and rockslides and runaway teams and quick-shooting road agents.

Veach, though, frankly enjoyed his work. He took pride in careful booking and scheduling that would give his employers the best return on their money. He was proud of the responsibility that was his in overseeing the maintenance of the big freight wagons and the well-being of the draft animals. It was his job to ensure the quality of the feed made available to each animal and the reliability of the hostler who tended them. It was his responsibility to send a rig to the wheelwright *before* a tire might fail or a spoke collapse.

Not many people knew or wanted to know how much expertise was needed to anticipate maintenance needs while at the same time being careful to avoid overspending on repairs that were not necessary. Nor would they likely appreciate the complexities of freight routing, he felt. Not that he would be much concerned with that himself in the near future, not until the line could be expanded to link more camps into a back-and-forth web of moving traffic. For the time being it would be simple point-to-point hauling.

He was tempted to explain this and more in the face of Jimbo Fyle's interest, but in response to the man's question he said only, "We'll haul in a bit of everything a man needs to live or work or have some merriment in the camps, and we'll haul out anything they want to send. More of it in than out, of course, on my end of it. Just the other way around on Whacker's end. You know."

Jimbo nodded happily. " 'Deed I do. I have a likin' for freighters, see." He brightened even more. "Say now, do we ever get over your way me an' Bo Jim might just stop in — to visit, like — an' see could you use a shotgun messenger or somethin'." He laughed. "I think we'd be kinda good at that, b'damn. I surely do."

Veach could not imagine himself trusting a shipment of any value at all to Jimbo Fyle or to Bo Jim Hatch, but he smiled pleasantly and said, "Of course I'd be glad to introduce you to Whacker. All the hiring will be up to him, naturally." In fact it would not. "And messengers have to be bonded, of course. I'm sure he'd be glad to talk to you about it."

"Damned if we mightn't just do it too, boy." Fyle tilted back in his chair and roared with laughter. Even Hatch seemed distantly amused. Both Warings remained isolated inside shells of discomfort. John Waring winced slightly at the loud laughter. His wife gave no sign of having heard it.

Veach continued with his preparation of their meal. For the first time in several days he was warmed by anticipation of the future. He was more than ever anxious now to resume his travel and meet Whacker. He hoped the delay would not force his friend to take on someone else instead.

The meal was skimpy enough, but alarming in how deeply it cut into their thin reserves. Veach had not felt free to dig into more than the few things he had brought with him. He used the dried beans he had carried and the last remnants of his salt pork, scarcely enough to add a hint of flavor to the beans. Even had he wanted to add meat to it he did not know where he could have found any. Apparently the bit of boiled meat he had shared the night he arrived was the last the Warings had had in their home. And somehow he did not want to touch the little Fyle had carried.

They ate in silence, Fyle concentrating on his food and none of the others in a mood for conversation. When they were done Ann Waring woodenly collected the soiled bowls and spoons. Bo Jim Hatch got quickly to his feet to bring in wash water. He did not ask for Fyle's approval this time before he left.

As Hatch left the tiny cabin Fyle gave him a look that Veach thought might have been annoyance. He corrected himself, however. He did not think Jimbo Fyle was likely to suffer any annoyance without proclaiming it aloud. Veach decided that he must have been mistaken.

Soon afterward, all four men stood coughing in the bitter cold outside while they waited for Ann Waring to prepare herself for the night. Their mood was far from companionable and each stood alone, although they stood in a tight group near the mule shelter. Fyle was the only one among them who paid attention to anything beyond the trampled snow under their feet. His eyes were constantly ranging over the gorge rim above them. Far too quickly he said, "That oughta be long enough."

"Not quite yet," Waring said.

"It's too cold to stand around out here," Fyle complained.

"Another minute or two won't hurt," Veach offered.

"Well I ain't so polite as you fancy boys," Fyle said, "an' I've had about enough of freezin' my butt just so's your woman can act the lady, dammit. She's human the same as we are an' I don't fancy much more of this bein' cold just so she can pretend she ain't the same as anybody else."

"Mr. Fyle," Waring said softly, "my wife *is* a lady. It is no pretense, sir."

Fyle turned menacingly to face the smaller man, but was interrupted by Bo Jim Hatch's touch at his elbow. "She really is a lady, ain't she, Jimbo?" the huge man asked. There was an oddly wondering innocence in his tone.

"Huh?" Fyle responded distractedly.

"I asked . . ."

"Oh hell, I heard you the first time. Yeah. Maybe. But I tol' you not to pay no attention, didn't I? Didn't I?"

"I guess you did, Jimbo," Hatch said unhappily. "Yeah, I guess you did. But ladies. They're special, Jimbo. Everybody knows that. Aren't they?"

"Yeah, sure. Now shut up an' do like you're told." He seemed to have forgotten Waring. He shoved his hands into the pockets of his parka and stared morosely at the snow-covered ground.

After a moment Waring said, "I think we can go inside now."

Fyle grunted. The others merely turned toward the cabin. Ann Waring was out of

185

view behind the drawn blankets when they returned.

CHAPTER 16

Veach was weary. His was not the satisfied tiredness of hard work or long travel when at least there was a sense of accomplishment underlying the fatigue. This was the vaguely depressing weariness of inactivity coupled with the loss of sleep he had suffered the night before. His eyes burned and his head ached from that and from the closeness and the increasing odors within the cabin, but even so he found he could not immediately claim sleep.

He lay awake for what seemed a long time, his eyes closed but his other senses acutely aware of the presence of others so close around him. From the sounds they made he gathered they had fallen quickly asleep. There certainly was no creak of bunk ropes overhead. John and Ann Waring were either sleeping or lying coldly silent beside each other rather than shifting and turning to accommodate a mutual warmth and closeness in the bunk they shared. Veach found himself wondering about them — about her — and still held those unwelcome thoughts in his mind when finally he slept.

He awakened in the morning sore from sleeping on packed earth, and with an aching sense of urgent discomfort in his loins. A hard floor, he decided, was a poor substitute for even the meanest rooming-house bed or for so little as untrodden dirt with grass or fallen needles to offer a measure of softness. For a moment he felt overwhelmed by a desire to leave this cabin and the isolated place where it stood. For that brief instant he would have risked anything, or nearly anything, for the chance to reach the pleasures and the comforts of town and job.

Veach sat up and shook his head violently from side to side as if he could physically shake such desires from his mind. They were unreasonable, and Veach liked to consider himself to be a reasonable man. He forced himself to accept the situation as it was and not as he would like it to be. After a moment the sense of being near a precipice of fear, even panic, began to subside.

Still, he wanted to leave the cabin, if only for a matter of minutes. He had no idea of the time, no way to judge if the sun was not yet risen or was already past the high, indented wall of the gorge downstream. Inside the cabin it was perpetually night when the lamp was extinguished, or it could be unending day for as long as they had oil to burn or wood for the stove.

Quietly Veach laid his blanket aside and pulled his boots over soiled, sweat-clammy socks. He pushed himself upright and padded on the balls of his feet to the wall pegs where his coat and hat were hung. He found his own garments by feel and pulled them on before he moved sideways toward the doorway where Bo Jim Hatch slept.

One boot toe scraped against Hatch's extended leg, and instantly the man was awake. He sat upright with a muffled grunt of alarm. Veach could feel and could hear the man's motion more than he could see it.

"I just want outside a minute," Veach whispered quickly.

"Huh?" Hatch's mumbled reply was sleep-fogged and thick.

Veach knelt beside him. Again he whispered. "I just want outside for a minute. Need some fresh air."

"Izit time to get up?"

"I don't think so. Maybe. Let me out now, okay?"

"You ain't going anyplace?"

"Just outside for some air."

"Yeah, all right." Veach could feel Hatch moving past him in the darkness. The smaller man stood and waited a moment. He could not see if Hatch was clear of the door.

He fumbled for the door latch and lifted it, then eased the door open and slipped through the briefly opened gap. It was like leaving a warm bed to dive directly into a pool of icy water.

It was not yet dawn, but the cloudless sky and springwater clarity of the air made the sky a silver- and diamond-sparkled field of dark gray that contrasted sharply with the solid black of the gorge walls. There was no moon visible, but the stars gave enough light to lend shape and substance to the snow and the rock on the gorge floor.

The cold was the worst Veach had felt in a long time, certainly the worst he had ever experienced while being so poorly prepared for cold weather in both his clothing and his intake of food. A proper breakfast or dinner could keep a man warm for half a day, it seemed. And a heavy coat and muffler would have made an immeasurable difference. He would have given a great deal for either. He settled for a deeply drawn sigh while he huddled as close as possible into his lightweight coat.

In spite of the cold, though, the air was clean and sweet outside the cabin, and he was glad to exchange the discomfort of the temperature for the temporary freedom of the open air. He breathed deeply, too deeply, and the cold clutched at his lungs. Unexpected pain lanced through his chest and for a moment he was racked by a spasm of dry coughing that could produce no phlegm. He straightened and rubbed the back of a glove across his lips.

A faint rattle behind him drew his attention toward the cabin. The door was pulled open and a heavily bundled figure emerged. There was enough light for him to see it was Bo Jim Hatch. The big man tested carefully to make sure the latch was securely tight behind him and then joined Veach. He shoved his hands into his coat pockets, but otherwise seemed not to notice the cold.

"Early yet," Hatch observed. His tone was agreeable, even pleasant.

Surprised by Bo Jim's inclination to talk, Veach blinked several times and peered closely at Hatch before he responded. But Hatch gave every appearance of being genuine. Veach doubted somehow that the man was capable of being devious or clever. "Couple hours 'til first light," Veach guessed.

Bo Jim grunted. He stood for a moment gazing down the gorge toward the east, toward the coming daylight. He watched for a time, then turned slowly and scanned both gorge walls before he again looked toward Veach. He seemed satisfied by the little he had been able to see.

"I like that lady," Hatch said abruptly. The declaration startled Veach to the extent that thought of the cold air was wiped away and he was unaware of physical discomfort. A moment earlier he had been suffering from the cold. Bo Jim Hatch, for his part, seemed completely matter-of-fact about his comment.

"You like her," Veach repeated, at a loss for words. He felt quite stupid at that moment, and his response did not make him feel brighter.

"Yes," Bo Jim said. "An' she likes me too. She said I look nice. You heard that. Didn't you hear her say that? A real lady, and that's what she said." He turned to stare at Veach, the stubborn set of his jaw and the unyielding directness of his gaze demanding that Veach confirm his statement.

"Yes," Veach agreed. "I heard her say it."

"Uh-huh. Jimbo heard it too." He paused. "Why'd Jimbo tell me not to pay her no mind then?"

Hatch sounded so puzzled, his tone suddenly so injured and uncertain, that Veach wondered if this was what Hatch had come out into the cold for.

"What do you think?" Veach countered.

Hatch looked annoyed. "I dunno. I wouldn't of asked you if I already knowed."

"Um . . . yeah, well, that makes sense."

Bo Jim nodded. His directness and basic simplicity again seemed to approach innocence despite his preoccupation with the woman — with the "lady." He spoke the word almost with reverence, as of something beyond him and beyond his understanding, as of a superior being and not merely a female human. Veach found the tone odd coming from Bo Jim, but undeniable. He wished he knew what dimly understood things might go on within the big man's mind.

"So why'd Jimbo say that?" Bo Jim persisted.

Veach shivered uncomfortably and made another pass under his nose with the icy leather of a thin glove. "Maybe because she's married," he said, not knowing what else he could tell the man.

"Aw, it couldn't be that. She *likes* me. You said so yourself. An' her man don't count for nothing hardly, little fella like him. Don't even carry a gun. Maybe don't even have one, a fella like that. You couldn't count him for anything."

The man's tone was level, serious, reasonable. That bothered Veach more than the words Hatch spoke. Bo Jim Hatch seemed genuinely not to recognize marriage or the presence of a husband as a deterring factor if John Waring was not powerful enough to present a physical barrier between Hatch and the woman. And Bo Jim seemed — on the basis of one compliment — to be equally certain that Ann Waring's inclination would be to accept his attentions. Veach wondered what those attentions might include. He was afraid he already knew.

"Mrs. Waring is a lady, Bo Jim," he parroted back to Hatch.

"Ain't she though?" he agreed happily. "I guess she's the first real lady I've knowed. She's nicer than some old hoor. Cleaner too, I bet. She doesn't smell bad or anything. Are all ladies like that?"

"Yes, I think they are." He could think of no better response. Veach wished Jimbo Fyle was awake to end this conversation.

"Somebody told me once that ladies don't sweat an' they don't ever lie neither," Hatch mused.

"I've heard that." Veach felt as if he was about to begin sweating himself. "Look, Bo Jim, you don't want to get in trouble with Jimbo, do you?"

"No, I wouldn't want to do that," he said solemnly.

"Right!" Veach declared with a small measure of relief. "And you know he'll be awfully mad if you don't do what he says. The best thing would be for you to do like he wants and not pay any more attention to Mrs. Waring. Jimbo knows what he's doing, you know."

"He's smart, that's for sure. Real smart. He always figures things out, even when I go and mess us up." Hatch sighed. "I get us in trouble sometimes." More brightly he added, "But Jimbo always figures a way out. Why, I haven't been a day in jail since me an' Jimbo took up together. Not one day."

Curiosity overcoming reluctance, Veach could not help asking, "You've been in jail before, then?"

"Oh sure. Lots of times. It ain't at all bad, you know. They feed you every day, not too bad most places, an' pretty soon they let you out. I can't see why there's some people gets so fussed up about it. Jimbo, now, he swears he'd die if somebody put him in a cage." He shrugged his shoulders. "Don't know why he'd feel like that, but he does. I've tried to tell him it ain't bad. They always let you out after a while."

Veach shuddered. The man sounded totally sincere. "I'm getting kind of cold," Veach said. "I guess I'll go back inside."

"Yeah," Hatch agreed, but he sounded as if the idea of physical discomfort was an abstraction that was beyond his experience.

"Listen, Bo Jim. I hope you'll do what Jimbo says and leave Mrs. Waring alone. I hope you won't get Jimbo mad at you."

Hatch turned to directly face Veach. He loomed above the smaller man, his expression set and hard, although his voice when he spoke was without emotion. "*You* wouldn't be telling me what to do, would you?"

"No!" Veach said quickly. "Not at all, Bo Jim. I like you too, see. I just don't want to see you getting into trouble with Jimbo. That's all."

Hatch nodded and turned back toward the cabin. Veach followed, and the shiver he felt now was caused by more than the temperature.

CHAPTER 17

Although the fire in the belly of the stove had long since died, the relative warmth of the cabin was comforting. Veach stripped off his coat and gloves and felt his way cautiously back to his bedding. He lay down and wrapped a blanket around him and dozed fitfully as he waited for morning.

As soon as the others were awake and Fyle had the fire relighted, Veach took John Waring by the elbow. "Let's get those animals out to the forage, Waring."

"In a moment." Waring rubbed at his eyes and smoothed sleep-tousled hair back from his forehead. "Give me a minute to wake up first."

"I really think we should get them out now," Veach insisted. He tugged impatiently at the man's sleeve.

"You're hell for bein' impatient this morning, ain't you?" Fyle observed from his chair nearest the stove. He leaned back contentedly and scratched himself. Behind him the fire grumbled briefly and settled into a steady purr as the flames reached a balanced draw. Bo Jim Hatch was in his usual position beside the doorway. Veach wondered if he had moved since the two of them entered the cabin several hours earlier.

Waring seemed to catch some of Veach's urgency. He had opened his mouth to protest being dragged so abruptly from bed to barn, but he closed it again without speaking. He pulled his boots on and took his coat and muffler from the wall.

Veach led the way outside, hoping as he did so that Hatch would not make any connection between their talk and Veach's present desire to take Waring out of hearing.

Off and on for the past two hours Veach had wondered whether he should tell Waring what Hatch had said. He did not know the man well enough to be sure of his reaction when he learned of Bo Jim's interest in his wife. An outburst of anger could lead anywhere, quite possibly to bloodshed, and Veach would not relish the thought of facing Hatch and Fyle even if they had not been armed.

Still it was only right, he decided, that Waring be warned so that he could do whatever might be possible to protect his wife. If the man did own a gun this might be a good time for him to place it close to hand. Veach did not feel he could put the burden of the woman's safety on a blind assumption that Bo Jim Hatch would continue to do as his partner told him.

If the temperature had moderated with the early morning sunlight it was too small a change to be felt. Veach felt the cold wash over and through him as soon as they were outdoors. The air seared their lungs and noses and turned their exhaled breath into hanging puffs of condensation.

Veach headed at a brisk walk toward the mule shed, the exercise doing little to create a sense of warmth under his thin coat. He wanted Waring well away from the cabin walls before they spoke.

Waring trailed behind more slowly. He was still logy with sleep, despite the sharp bite of the cold that crept under the bottom of his coat and already pinched at his cheeks and ears. He shoved his hands deep into his coat pockets, yawned and rolled his head to loosen tight shoulder and neck muscles.

"My God! Look there," Waring blurted. He ran ahead and grabbed Veach by the arm. He was pointing up the gorge floor toward a dark shape crumpled on the stark white of the frozen snow.

"That's a man out there." Both broke into a floundering run through shin-deep snow. The exertion sent bitterly cold air rasping through their chests like a succession of knife-edged saw blades, but they held the pace for the several hundred yards that had separated them from the fallen figure. By the time they reached the man both were heaving for breath, their legs cramped with pain and feeling as if they were sheathed with soft, flexible lead plating.

Waring reached him first. For a moment he stood over the man with trembling legs spraddled, bending while he drew in raw gulps of the too-cold air. Veach stumbled to a halt beside him and dropped to his knees next to the unconscious figure. Veach took hold of the man's jaw and turned his head toward them.

"Is he . . . alive?" Waring gasped.

Veach nodded. He did not want to attempt speech yet. After a moment he said, "Yeah . . . think so . . . just barely."

Waring straightened and looked back along the erratic path of trampled snow where the man had walked. A number of wider depressions showed where he had fallen but had managed to drive himself back onto his feet.

The man was gaunt and pale beneath perhaps a week's growth of beard. He appeared to be young, not long out of his teens. The brim of his hat had been tied down over his ears. His eyes were closed, the lower lashes coated with ice where the intense cold had pulled tears onto his cheeks. His lips were parted, drawn back thin and tight, pale now with a faintly purplish cast under the flesh surface. Collected moisture from his breath had formed a crust of ice around his mouth and on the ends of his high-turned coat collar.

"Do you know him?"

Waring shook his head. "He hasn't been by here before. He must have been coming down from the Idaho side."

Veach was rubbing at the man's cheeks without drawing any sign of consciousness. "Makes no difference anyhow, I guess. We got to get him inside or he's got no chance at all. Maybe doesn't anyway."

Together they draped the man's arms over their shoulders and rose with the limp form suspended between them. There was no reflexive attempt to support himself or to walk with them when they began to drag him back the way they had come. The toes of his boots dug long, wavering furrows in the snow behind them.

Keeping him upright was awkward. The bulk of clothing between them made getting a firm grip difficult, and the cold was already driving the sense of feeling from hands that needed fading strength.

"My God but he's heavy for a scrawny fellow," Veach said. Waring did not bother to reply. He was in better physical condition than Veach, yet the cold and exertion and lack of food were telling heavily on him. They passed the animal shelter, grateful that the bed and the stove were now only paces away.

The cabin door opened as they came near, and Fyle and Bo Jim stepped outside. Fyle's eyes narrowed when he saw the man they were supporting. "Who the hell is that?"

"No idea," Veach said. "Found him in the snow."

Fyle motioned Hatch toward the injured man. Bo Jim took him from the straining Waring and Veach without effort, picking him up as easily as a child carries a large doll. Jimbo held the door open for them to pass.

Ann Waring was just emerging from behind the blanket screen, her hair disheveled and her dress only partially buttoned. When she saw the unconscious man her eyes widened in alarm and one hand flew to her throat. She recovered quickly, though, and hurried forward, forgetting her appearance. She laid a hand against the man's cold cheek and, looking up at Bo Jim, said, "Put him on our bed please, Mr. Hatch."

For a moment Bo Jim failed to respond. He stood holding the nearly frozen man and staring down the partly opened front of the woman's dress.

"Do it," Jimbo snapped.

Bo Jim elbowed the hanging blankets aside and placed the man onto the Warings' unmade bed. As soon as he straightened, Ann Waring slid in front of him to sit beside the unconscious form on her bed.

She cupped the man's face in her hands and said, "He's so cold." Giving her husband a frightened look over her shoulder she asked, "Are you sure he's alive?"

"He was a minute ago," Waring assured her.

Veach had gone to the stove. He spilled the last water from the bucket into a pan and held the bucket out behind him. When no one took it he turned impatiently and thrust the empty bucket into Fyle's belly. Fyle was standing nearest to him. "We'll need more," he said. "Gotta give him a warm bath. Rub him down. Get some blood to moving."

Jimbo grunted and stared for a moment into the empty bucket. He gave Veach a dark look, but reached out to take Hatch by the arm. "Fill this thing an' get back in here," he ordered.

The Warings were both seated on the edge of the bed, the woman rubbing at the man's cheeks while John Waring fumbled open the buttons of the stranger's coat. Already the warmth of the cabin was causing packed snow on his clothing to melt soddenly onto the rumpled blankets. Rolling and tugging at the limp figure, they managed to pull his coat and trousers off, but still found no response to their efforts.

"He's pretty far gone," Waring said.

Veach plunged a finger into the pan on the stove, then stooped to add more fuel to the firebox. "This is starting to warm. You don't want it real hot anyhow."

"Bring that pan, Mr. Veach," the woman said. "We can heat more when Mr. Hatch returns."

John Waring finished stripping away the man's outer clothing while his wife found a rag to dip into the lukewarm water. She began bathing his face and chest with the wet rag, paying no attention to the moisture that ran onto her blankets.

"Is this doing any good at all, John?"

Waring had found another scrap of cloth and was washing the man's feet with slightly warm water. His toes were almost without color, dirty nails standing out against whitish flesh. "I hope so, dear. He is still breathing, isn't he?"

"I think so."

Veach moved nearer and bent to examine the man more closely. A hint of pulsebeat thumped weakly in the hollow of his throat, a flutter almost too faint to be seen. "He's alive all right, but not by much."

Jimbo Fyle was standing back with his arms folded. He had an expression of watchful interest, but he showed no particular anxiety for the welfare of the nearly frozen visitor. He seemed more curious than concerned. Fyle turned when he heard the rattle of the door latch as Bo Jim Hatch let himself into the cabin.

"Fill a pot an' set it on t' heat," Fyle ordered.

Bo Jim nodded. He set the bucket down and tested to see that the latch was securely shut before he retrieved the pail and crossed to the stove. The Warings had only one pot large enough to hold the entire bucketful of water. Hatch filled it and placed it on the center of the stove surface. "Should I get more, Jimbo?"

"Huh?"

"The bucket, Jimbo. Do you want I should fill it again? It's empty. See?" He held the bucket for Fyle's inspection.

"You do that, Bo. We'll be needin' more. You jus' do that." He waved Bo Jim away and turned back toward the Warings. Fyle turned too soon to see the look of annoyance that fleetingly crossed Bo Jim Hatch's face.

"What can I do?" Veach asked.

"It might help if you worked on his hands," Waring suggested. "If they are as bad as his feet he may lose them."

Veach sat at the man's head and cupped one stiff hand between his palms. Fyle continued to hang back and observe what the others were doing.

"My God," Veach said, "the fellow's hands are as cold as the snow, I think. The fingers don't want to bend or anything."

"We have no experience with this, Mr. Veach," Ann Waring said. She looked distressed. "Have you?"

"No, ma'am, I'm afraid not. Not with anything real serious, and I'm afraid this boy is in as serious a shape as a live man could be."

"Mr. Fyle?" she persisted.

Fyle shrugged. When he did Veach noticed

anew how massive his shoulders were. He gave the impression that he could have chosen to drive the freezing cold from the man's body by sheer force of will, but he said, "Enough to know he's gonna die. You're wastin' your time, little lady. That boy won't live out the night."

"*I* think we can save him," Waring said. "He has a strong will to live or he wouldn't be here now. With proper attention he should have a good chance of recovery." Waring was talking more to his wife than to Jimbo Fyle. The encouragement drew from her a weak smile.

"Suit yourself," Fyle said.

"We shall," Waring assured him firmly. "I don't suppose you would care to offer any suggestions, Fyle? I mean, you *do* claim to have some experience with freezing, even if you feel this is a losing cause."

Again Fyle shrugged. "You're doing all right."

After more than an hour the man remained unconscious, although splotches of color had returned to his cheeks. Waring sat upright and arched his back to ease muscles strained from bending. "I think we should cover him now," he said. "Perhaps heat some rocks and lay them under the blankets. I can't think of anything else at this point.

Put the covers over him, Ann. Veach and I will bring you the rocks. There are some loose pieces at the front of the shed." He stood and reached for his coat. His wife drew the bedding over the still form, hesitated, then began taking down the blankets that had been hung as curtains between the bed and the rest of the single room.

Veach glanced into the back corners of the cabin where the stone walls met the rock face of the gorge wall. Much of the loose rock in the corners looked to be piled and mortared poorly, if at all. Jimbo Fyle remained in his seat, looking toward the woman and the man on the bunk. Veach hoped he would not notice Waring's decision to bring frozen rocks in from outdoors instead of using already-warm materials close at hand. That must be where Waring kept the gold he had dug.

CHAPTER 18

Veach's horse nickered eagerly as they approached the shed. It stood at the barred doorway blowing jets of frozen condensation into the open air. The mules were huddled together in the far back corner of the structure. Collected moisture from their bodies and breath had formed a slick film of ice on the rock there.

"This keeps up much longer and those animals are going to be too poor to use when we do get a chance to make a run out of here," Veach said.

"They seem no worse than Fyle's," Waring observed.

"No. Hell, there's not much of anything for them to eat anyhow. Listen, John, if that fella could get in here on foot maybe a horse could get out. Besides, maybe that youngster wasn't alone. I think one of us should back-trail him. I, uh, I'll go myself, but I'd like to borrow something warmer than this coat. It isn't much protection in weather like this."

"He might have been on the floor already. Fyle and Hatch were, you know. And if anyone was with him they are probably dead now. You know that, don't you?"

Veach nodded. He picked up an armload of water-rounded rocks from the shed front. "I've thought of that. It's an awful slim possibility, but I think we should take a look. 'Specially if there could be somebody still out there."

"A man alone in this cold . . ." Waring's voice tailed away. He shook his head. "Fighting drifted snow can pull the strength right out of a person. You could get a few miles upstream and not be able to get back. I don't like the idea. Not at all."

Veach gave him a look of surprise. "Hell, man, you can't go with me and leave your missus alone here. And somebody *has* to go. There could be people out there needing help an' if they do they'll need it right now."

Again Waring shook his head stubbornly.

Without thinking Veach said, "It's practically like you don't want to be left alone here with those two."

"One man alone . . . something could happen. You never know." From the anguished look that came into Waring's eyes Veach realized that the man *was* afraid to be left alone if something should happen to Veach while he was out in the bitter weather. Yet Waring's basic humanity was making him ashamed of this impulse to protect his wife and himself, perhaps at the expense of someone else in greater need. He was not meeting Veach's eyes now.

"What about Bo Jim?" Waring blurted.

"What?"

"Bo Jim Hatch," Waring said. "He could go with you. Two men working together would be ten times safer than a man alone. Well, why couldn't Hatch go with you? Frankly, I wouldn't trust Fyle and Hatch together even if they would go. But why not you and Hatch?"

Veach bobbed his head abruptly in quick agreement. "I hadn't thought of ol' Bo Jim for some reason, but yeah, that would be all right, I think." He looked at the horse shoving its muzzle hungrily past the barred shed opening. "Look, Bo Jim and me can go together. On foot, I guess. We won't go far anyway, and we could use up the horses before we really need them if we aren't careful. But we could go afoot. The two of us would be all right that way. Save the horses for later. What do you think?"

When he got a nod of agreement from

Waring, Veach removed the bars from the doorway. The roan horse bolted forward immediately and broke into a lumbering canter toward the other horses downstream on the gorge floor. The mules followed more slowly, pausing to sniff at the snow cover and placing their feet with delicate precision. All of the animals showed rib-lines on their sides despite the thickness of their winter coats.

"They don't look too awful bad yet," Veach lied to himself. Neither he nor John Waring could believe that. The livestock were not finding enough forage to maintain their body weight in such extreme weather.

"We had best get these inside," Waring said.

"Sure."

They carried their loads of rock back into the cabin and opened their coats to the welcome heat before they placed the cold stones onto the stove top. Condensation quickly began to form and to drop, sizzling and dancing, onto the hot sheet iron of the stove.

"Is he any better?" Waring asked.

His wife shook her head. "No change at all, John."

"Don't expect none," Fyle advised cheerfully. "He won't come out o' that."

"You take that calmly enough," Waring told him. His expression was mild, but a sharp edge of annoyance touched his voice.

Fyle shrugged. In a matter-of-fact tone he said, "The kid don't mean anything to me, Johnny. Never seen him before an' you didn't neither. Hell, if he lives we just gotta feed him. Better for us if he don't."

"That is a damned poor attitude for a man to take," Waring said testily. "What if it were you lying there in need of help?"

"The point is, Johnny, it ain't me." Fyle grinned. "Besides, nothin' bad ever happens to me an' Bo Jim. Does it, Bo?" He glanced briefly toward Hatch's doorside place on the floor.

"That's true, Jimbo," Bo Jim said solemnly. "Ever since you an' me been together it's been true. Gospel."

"None of which makes the least difference," Ann Waring interjected. "The fact is that this young man *is* alive, and we shall tend to his needs as well as we can. There certainly is no need for anyone to argue about it. Are those rocks hot yet, John?"

Waring turned, but Veach, still warming himself by the stove, laid a hand on one of the stones and said, "No, ma'am, they have a good ways to go yet to heat up this first time. It's awful cold out there."

The woman nodded. "Let me know when they are ready, please." She smoothed the blankets over the still form of the unconscious man and tugged them higher and closer under his chin.

Fyle grinned wickedly. "There's a quicker way'n that, little lady," he said. Veach looked at him angrily, but Jimbo's attention was on the woman. Veach glanced at Bo Jim in time to see the man's eyes widen with what might have been sudden hunger.

"Yes?" the woman asked.

Jimbo laughed with delight that she had taken his bait. "You jus' crawl right in next to him an' warm him up your own self, little lady."

Waring wheeled to face the much larger man. "Shut your damned mouth," he snapped. His face was drained of color and his jaw muscles were set. Jimbo laughed all the louder.

It was obvious that Waring was fighting for control of himself — for his wife's sake — and losing. He added as he listened to Fyle's laughter, "You can treat my wife with respect instead of acting like a pig, like some kind of scum."

Fyle's eyes hardened. His laughter was cut abruptly short. He rose from his chair and loomed menacingly over Waring. "It's you better keep your mouth shut, you pipsqueak little son of a bitch, or I'll show you some scum." He reached toward Waring's shirt-front.

Ann Waring jumped from the side of the bed and squeezed herself between the two men. She grabbed Fyle's hand in both of hers and clung to it. "Please!" To her husband she desperately said, "It's all right, John. Mr. Fyle was making a joke. Just a joke. That's all, dear." Her head swiveled quickly and tilted far back so she could peer up at Fyle. "I know you meant nothing improper, Mr. Fyle. And my husband was only expressing his concern for me. Now please . . . both of you . . . sit down. There is no need for this. Please."

She shoved Fyle on the chest, and he allowed himself to be moved back into his seat. Waring stood braced and rigid until she took him by the arm and tugged him into a sitting position on the edge of their bunk.

Beside the stove Veach let out a breath he had been holding too long. His hand felt cramped and he looked at it. He was surprised to see that he was clutching one of the rocks that had been on the stove top. He did not remember grabbing it. Surreptitiously he returned it to its place, careful to

215

not let the stone clank against metal as he did so. He had been watching Waring and Jimbo Fyle during the brief outburst, but wished now that he had had the presence of mind to watch Bo Jim instead. To judge from Hatch's posture and expression now there might have been nothing of interest taking place in the cabin since their arrival.

Ann Waring gave her husband and then Fyle a weak smile. She sat beside Waring and took his hand, holding it tightly between hers.

Fyle leaned back in his chair and folded his arms. He looked benignly from one Waring to the other. To the woman he said, "Little lady, I never will understand just how it is a good lookin' little ol' gal can go an' get herself tied up with a little bit of a fella like your man." He shook his head and grinned, deliberately insulting. "Nope. Not when there's real men roaming around lookin' for women, I can't."

Her hands tightened on Waring's until the flesh of her fingers whitened, but he gave no sign he felt the pressure nor that he had heard Fyle's remarks. There was no danger of him losing control of himself over that. Not when the comments were directed toward him rather than his wife.

"It amazes me as well, Mr. Fyle," Waring

said mildly. He turned to look at his woman. "But it never ceases to please me."

Veach cleared his throat loudly. "I think these rocks should be warm enough to do some good now." In truth they were barely warm, but Veach gathered half of them from the stove regardless. "If you'd pull those blankets down, ma'am . . ." His handling of the rocks to place each one was more than consideration. Veach did not want her to touch the nearly cold rocks.

"Of course, Mr. Veach." She quickly stood and stripped the heavy layers of bedding back from their unconscious guest. The man had not moved since they placed him on the bunk.

Veach bent and began laying muskmelon-size rocks along the man's sides. As he did one slipped from his arm and fell onto the bunk.

"Here, let me help," Ann Waring said quickly. She took the rock and began to move it toward her patient. She hesitated when she touched the cool stone, her eyes locking onto Veach's. After the briefest pause she blinked and smiled. "Thank you, Mr. Veach," she said.

"Yes, ma'am. We, uh, can replace these with warmer ones in a minute or two."

"Yes, that will be fine." She flipped the

blankets forward and tucked them tightly around the man. She turned and forced a cheerful smile. "Now, Mr. Fyle. How would you feel about a bite of lunch?"

CHAPTER 19

They were eating too much. Veach knew
they were. He could do nothing to control
it, and there seemed to be nothing Waring
could do either. Judging from Waring's
expression, the man resented every mouthful of food his wife prepared, particularly
the quantities that went to Jimbo Fyle. Had
it not been for Fyle they could have weath-
ered over in far greater safety than was now
possible.

Veach hunched over the table and concentrated on the bland food set before them.
Normally he would have been hesitant to
take helpings as large as those so freely
taken by Fyle and Bo Jim Hatch. Now, in
anticipation of a possibly long exposure to
the outdoor temperatures, he matched Fyle
spoon for spoon, piling on the lumpy mush
the woman had prepared. What they needed
to fight the cold, though, was fat. He wished
she had cooked the rest of Fyle's bacon or

at least used some grease to flavor the corn-meal.

At least they had coffee. Veach poured himself a second cup before Fyle had time to finish his first helping. He did not want the pot to run dry before he got his refill. The coffee was by far the best part of the meal. He felt fleetingly sorry for John Waring, but sneaked a brief glance at the woman as a reminder and smiled to himself. The man could always hire his cooking done, he decided.

"Is everything all right, gentlemen?" Ann Waring asked.

"Yes, ma'am," Veach dutifully mumbled. Neither Fyle nor Hatch responded at all. Waring's praise was quickly offered, but Veach thought the words sounded mechanical and dull, like a line of poetry recited by rote after repetition to a point where the original meaning had been lost. Like singing "amen" at the end of a hymn. Someone — it must have been a preacher — had told him once that that was a word meaning you were affirming the truth of all that had been said before, but that no one used it as such any longer. It was just a way to end the song or the prayer or whatever. The meaning no longer seemed to matter. You just said it and it was expected of you and once you said it everyone was satisfied. That was just the way Waring's praise came out now, Veach thought. Neither Waring nor his wife listened to the words or paid attention to the meaning. The fact of saying them was a habit for both people. That was all right, Veach decided. It satisfied them.

Bo Jim left his nest by the door and came to the table to scrape the last of the mush into his bowl.

"We'll need your help as soon as the meal is over," Waring said to him.

Hatch stopped where he was and looked at Jimbo patiently and without a change in expression.

"An' what would you be needin' of ol' Bo Jim, I ask you?"

Waring gave Fyle a look of annoyance that was quickly altered with a flicker of a wry smile. "What with one thing and another," he said, "I almost forgot, but Mr. Veach and I were talking outside. We think someone should follow the tracks left by that young man over there." He angled his head toward the unconscious form on the bunk.

"You do, huh? Well I can't see no need for it."

"He might have been with others. There could be someone in need of our help."

"The rest o' them are dead now," Fyle

221

said with certainty.

"Them?" Waring asked. Fyle had sounded as if he knew there were others.

Jimbo smiled easily. "A man don't travel this country alone."

"I was," Veach said softly.

Fyle's smile expanded into a grin. He leaned back away from the table. "Just shows you ain't as bright as you oughta be. Man oughta know better, this time o' year."

Waring shook his head impatiently. "That is beside the point, Mr. Fyle. The fact is, someone *could* need our help. Or, doubtful though it may seem, that man over there may have cleared a path we could use to get out of here. Whatever the truth is, we need to know it."

"Not worth the risk," Jimbo said emphatically. "You 'specially don't need t' send my partner out to do your runnin'. If you wanta look, Johnny, whyn't you jus' saddle up an' go? We'll wait right here. In case you come back, that is."

"Neither the horses nor the mules are strong enough to risk using them now," Waring reasoned. "Someone has to go on foot. And it can't be any one man. That would be much too dangerous. Veach volunteered to go. We suggest that Mr. Hatch accompany him."

Fyle did not take time to ponder it. "Nope," he said flatly.

Ann Waring pursed her lips. Hesitantly she said, "He might have left some food somewhere behind him. I mean, alone or in company . . . whatever . . . no one is going to travel here without carrying food, are they?"

Bo Jim stirred. "She's right, Jimbo. I seen . . ."

"Shut up, Bo Jim," Fyle snapped. The man did.

Veach looked up at Hatch. He wanted to ask what he had seen, but decided such a question would not be answered now and might well precipitate another argument with Jimbo Fyle.

"The little lady could be right about that. Prob'ly wouldn't hurt to take a little look. An' maybe Bo Jim *oughta* go along." He grinned insolently. "Jus' to make sure you boys stay honest about anything you find."

Waring colored slightly, but Veach had himself under control. He nodded patiently and said, "That's good enough reason." He wanted to add that it showed what they might expect from Fyle in the future, but he refrained. It was a thing better remembered than discussed, he decided.

"Eat up, Bo," Fyle ordered. "You'll be

goin' out in a minute."

Hatch carried the bowl back to his favored seat by the door.

Veach was almost warm. In addition to his own clothing he was wearing two sweaters borrowed from Waring, Waring's coat, a pair of gloves pulled over his own thin gloves and a long woolen muffler that Ann Waring had laced around his head in place of the hat he had left behind. It was the muffler, wrapped so only his nose and eyes were exposed, that made the greatest difference in comfort. With his belly nearly full and the warmth of the stove a recent memory on his ribs, only the cold seeping through the leather of his boots was still causing discomfort.

For a moment he cursed the sense of stylishness that had made him buy the narrow boots favored by the dashing cattle drovers who were stocking the northern ranges with Texas beef and imprinting both their dress and their openhanded, happy-go-lucky ways on those around them. There simply was not room inside the hand-cobbled, closely fitted boots to add extra layers of cloth, even though Waring had had spare socks to offer. For riding the boots were ideal. For floundering through deep, broken snow they were far from it.

Ahead of him Bo Jim Hatch's broad back surged forward seemingly without effort. Already the cold air was causing sharp knife-points of pain to explore the deeper recesses of Veach's lungs, and they had come as yet little distance beyond the point where he and Waring had found the fallen man.

The crust was already broken from the earlier passage through it and the snow cover was not so deep as to present an immediate problem. But the clinging drag against their feet gave a small but already perceptible increase to the effort of walking. They had to wade more than walk, and Veach could feel the effort in the long muscles of his calves and thighs. His feet were distinctly painful.

Hatch said nothing, nor did he pause to rest. He moved forward with machinelike, monotonous regularity, Veach trudging behind wishing the man's pace was not quite so steady nor so rapid.

Within the first two miles of moving west, upstream of the cabin, they passed three drifts that Ann Waring's nearly frozen patient had somehow broken through. The drifts were both deep and wide, and Veach could guess how much strength each would have drained away from the man. Relatively warm as he was and fresh from days of rest, the belly-deep, already breached drifts sapped Veach's strength and sent new lances of sharp pain through his limbs and deep into his lungs. The going was difficult even after the drifts had been broken and trampled by two men before him. For an exhausted and nearly frozen man traveling alone through the night, those windblown snow barriers would have been heartbreakingly difficult to pass. After the third of them Veach called out in a gasping voice, asking for a halt.

Bo Jim had broken out of the deep snow first and was already a dozen paces ahead and walking strongly. He stopped and turned to wait. Veach moved up to him and stopped, bent over at the waist with his hands braced on slightly bent knees. He tried to control his breathing so he could keep the frigid air from reaching his lungs before it had time to warm during its passage.

"You're sweating," Bo Jim accused. He sounded impatient. His voice betrayed no strain.

"I know." Veach sounded — and felt — apologetic for that fact, and that annoyed him more than the knowledge that Hatch was correct.

"It ain't good to sweat in th' cold," Bo Jim said. "Stop to rest now an' the sweat could freeze. That ain't good, man."

"I know," Veach said. And he did. There was no danger of chilling as long as they kept moving. It was now, when the cold could search beneath his sweat-dampened clothing, that the greatest danger came. "It isn't enough to worry about," he insisted.

"Your business," Hatch said.

"Yeah." Veach exhaled loudly and moved out of the trodden path to a snow hillock blown to rounded fullness in the lee of a scrubby clump of saltbush. He lowered himself onto and into it, letting the mound of snow serve as a chair.

Hatch looked at him without expression. "Freeze your butt doin' that," he observed.

"I know, dammit!" Veach snapped. He was feeling irritable, especially since Hatch was right in his warning. No sooner had he sat in the snow than the raw cold bled through the fabric of his trousers and the single layer of his borrowed long johns. Within seconds he felt as if he had sat naked on a cake of ice. Worse, he knew that his own body heat would melt the snow and saturate the cloth of his trousers with icy water. The water would remain to chill and to bother him after he stood. Veach felt tired and foolish and therefore angry.

"Man oughta take care in this kinda weather," Bo Jim said.

"Yeah, yeah, I know," Veach said wearily. Inwardly he acknowledged that Hatch was correct. With more effort than he wanted to give he regained his feet and reached back to brush the snow from the seat of his trousers. "So all right. Let's go."

Hatch nodded. He turned and began slogging forward through the path trampled once already by the man they had left in the cabin behind them.

They made another mile. The floor was narrower here, drifts more frequent. In spite of the path broken by the man who had come this way before them, the going was difficult. Veach could no longer feel his toes, and his legs were leaden. Even Hatch was moving more slowly, his breathing labored and his face darkened by the exertion of doing the heavier work of walking in the lead.

"We could use a break," Veach said.

Bo Jim shook his head. "No place here." He hunched his shoulders and continued doggedly forward.

"Just a rest. We don't have to have shelter."

Again Hatch shook his head. Veach muttered his annoyance, but continued to follow.

The gorge walls were pinching closer here, the floor continuing to narrow. They entered an area of drift snow that stretched hundreds of yards at or over the height of a man.

Veach plowed forward, wanting to pant for breath yet knowing that if he sucked the needed air into his lungs it would sear them with cold. He walked with his head down, using thigh muscles to lift and place feet he could barely find by feel.

Abruptly Bo Jim stopped. Veach, his eyes cast down, nearly walked into his back. He sighed as he thought about a rest stop. He wished there was a way to get warm too. The cold had long since penetrated the last layer of clothing. The cabin was miles behind.

Hatch turned and pulled at Veach's coat sleeve, tugging him forward. Bo Jim pointed upstream.

"I see something up there. Somethin' in the snow. You see it?"

"I do, man. Right up there."

Together they began to run laboriously through the deep softness of the broad drift, floundering and falling, but making the best speed they could.

Chapter 20

It was a horse, a ragged-coated bay, grotesque in frozen death. It lay flat, long neck extended and drawn straight and high to an angle impossible during life. Oddly pale lips were pulled back to expose blunt, yellow-streaked teeth. Hairs that would have been unnoticeable when the horse lived stood out starkly black now against the frozen flesh of lips and muzzle. Ice had crusted the animal's long lashes and had formed a skin across the one large, staring brown eye they could see. Once it had been a handsome animal. It was no longer. There were no tracks or other signs here of people except the man they had left in the cabin.

Tracks left in the snow showed that he had been leading the horse when it fell for the last time. It must have been a highly favored animal, Veach thought. According to the tracks, the man had broken trail for the horse as far as they could see the white-on-white trail ahead.

"Nothing else up there?" Veach asked. He could see nothing upstream from where they stood.

Bo Jim grunted. He stepped onto the snow-caked ribs of the dead horse for more elevation and a greater range of vision. Veach winced, although he knew the dead animal could not feel Bo Jim's heavy bootheels. "Nothin'," Hatch said.

"I suppose we should turn back now." Veach was more than willing to return to the warmth of the cabin. The search and a possible rescue had sounded fine when discussed indoors, beside a purring sheet metal stove and with his belly full of hot food. Here, miserably cold and with feet and now fingers painfully affected, the idea of going forward was not nearly so attractive. There was nothing ahead that they could see, and the drifts seemed to get worse, not better. They knew the drifts could be breached. They had been already by the man and the horse. But the cost of that travel was also apparent. The horse was dead. The man would have been by now if they had not found him.

Bo Jim Hatch grunted and stepped off the horse to the trampled snow. He bent and ripped the saddlebags away from behind the dead horse's cantle. Veach felt uneasy viewing such a violation of someone else's private belongings, but he knew it had to be done. If the man had had any food with him they would need it.

Hatch found some lint-speckled scraps of beef jerky. He crammed one into his mouth, handed Veach another and shoved the few remaining pieces into the deep side pocket of his coat.

The jerky was dry and cold and had no flavor. Veach chewed it mechanically, hoping it would warm and soften soon.

Bo Jim took a pouch from the saddlebags and shoved that into his pocket with the jerky. It looked like a leather snap purse, but Veach could not be sure from the fleeting glimpse he had. Hatch tossed the saddlebags into the snow.

"That's it, I guess," Veach said. He turned on feet that felt as awkward as tree stumps and began to move back the way they had come.

"No."

Veach stopped and looked back. "Why?"

Bo Jim pulled his knife. For an instant Veach felt a deeper chill than the weather could cause, but Hatch lowered himself ponderously to his knees in the deep snow beside the dead horse.

"What in the world are you doing, Bo Jim?"

Hatch looked at him blankly. "Th' lady wants more food."

"So?"

Bo Jim gouged the point of his knife into the flank of the horse. "The meat's still good."

"Yes. Yes, I guess it is." The meat would be nourishing, he knew. It was the idea of eating horseflesh that was somehow repugnant. By himself it simply would not have occurred to Veach to view a dead horse as a source of meat. Bo Jim Hatch seemed to have no such prejudices.

Bo Jim hacked roughly at the hindquarter. The tough hide and much of the meat were frozen and difficult to cut, but deeper into the flesh the meat was not yet solid. Hatch smiled to himself when he encountered the easier knife work. "Won't take long," he said.

Hatch cut away one large ham and took additional time to neatly bone it. He seemed impervious to the effects of the cold, although Veach was now acutely uncomfortable, stamping his feet and flailing his arms in an effort to warm himself. Carefully Bo Jim laid the ham aside and began to scoop snow away from the horse's back.

"*Now* what are you doing?" Veach asked impatiently.

Without pausing in his work Hatch said, "Gotta roll it over. Get to that other haunch, see?"

Veach shook his head irritably, but knelt to help remove snow so the carcass would roll more easily. He had long since decided that there was little that could be done to direct or to hurry the big, slow-moving Bo Jim once the man had set a task for himself.

The second cut was more difficult. The snow-buried quarter was solidly frozen nearly all the way through. Hatch worked at it patiently, his sharp knife slipping and gnawing but making progress, however slight, with each renewed cut. Veach wondered if the man's knees would not be affected from his kneeling so long in the snow. If they were, Bo Jim did not show it. He worked doggedly on. When he had the ham free he again took the time to cut the bone away. Finally Hatch stood and put his knife away.

The two hams Bo Jim had cut would weigh about thirty pounds apiece. Veach lifted one and was pleased with the amount of meat they would be able to take back, but found it to be an awkward burden even while standing still. Carrying it through deep snow would be even more difficult.

"We need some way to carry these," he said.

Bo Jim shrugged. He had the other piece of meat tucked under an arm as if it were a feather pillow. An ooze of not-quite-frozen blood darkened his coat.

"We could rig pack slings from that saddle blanket," Veach suggested. When he got no response from Hatch he laid the meat aside and bent to try to remove the saddle from the dead and now mutilated horse.

The cinch straps were secured in iron-solid knots. Sweat and snow once melted by fading body heat had now frozen in and on the leather latigos. Veach fumbled awkwardly at the front and rear knots without success. His gloved fingertips could gain no purchase on the straps, and he doubted that he would have done much better bare-handed even if his fingers had been warm. He muttered a short curse.

Bo Jim reached forward over his shoulder. His knife blade slashed twice, ripping through both the cinches and through recently live horsehide. Again Veach winced and felt stupid for doing so.

Veach shoved the saddle aside and yanked the blanket free. With Bo Jim's knife he cut and tore the blanket lengthwise and tied the ends of the two strips to form a pair of crude slings. Draped across their chests and adjusted for length, the slings held their burdens of meat at hip level and left their hands free.

"Is that better?" Veach asked when he was done.

Bo Jim gave him a delighted smile. "You're 'most as smart as Jimbo, I bet," he said. "You come up with that real clever-like." He seemed quite happy with the simple arrangement. "C'mon then. It won't be much past dark 'fore we get there."

Veach had not been paying attention to the time and was startled now to realize that the entire gorge floor was in shadow, with only a narrow strip of direct sunlight showing on a few of the higher upthrusts of ragged rock overhead. Not that they had to worry about getting lost. With the completely cloudless sky overhead and unbroken snow on each side of the trampled path they would not even need moonlight to find their way. But it would be even colder after dark.

"Lead the way," Veach said. The horse ham bumped uncomfortably at his hip and the sling gouged painfully into his shoulder despite the padding of coat and sweaters. He wished they were already within the protective warmth of the cabin walls.

■ ■ ■ ■

The stove just was not hot enough. Its heat seemed to strike his skin and be reflected away. The cold lay deeper than that, and the heat did not seem to reach it. He had shucked the coat and peeled the sweaters off, and it seemed to do no good.

Shakily Veach dug the toe of one boot into the heel of the other and kicked his boots off. If Jimbo Fyle had had any hint of consideration, he decided, the man would have moved to the other chair, but he did not. Veach hobbled on sock-footed pegs around to his own chair and sank onto it. He stripped his socks away and began rubbing at white, ugly toes he could feel only with his hands. There was no sensation coming from the toes themselves. Minutes later, when feeling did return, it was a faint tingle growing rapidly to a fierce burn so achingly deep that it was all he could do to keep from crying aloud.

Bo Jim Hatch seemed still unaffected. The only concession the man had made after removing his coat and returning to his door-side seat was to pull off his boots and wiggle his toes inside dirty, torn socks.

Ann Waring was using a rag and a bucket

237

of water to sponge clean the slabs of meat they had brought. Contact with the saddle blanket had deposited on them an unappetizing accumulation of horsehair and grime.

"How is your patient, John?" Veach asked after reporting what little they had found.

"It's hard to tell," Waring said. "He's still out, but I really think now he is sleeping rather than unconscious. I'd like to believe he will be all right."

"I feel sure of it, Mr. Veach," the woman said.

Fyle chuckled. He had seemed quite satisfied that Veach and Bo Jim brought back meat and nothing more. "You just oughta listen to ol' Jimbo, you ought. That'un is gonna die. Wait an' see if I'm right." He grinned. "But there's more to eat now, ain't there? See? Nothin' bad ever happens to Jimbo. Whyn't you fry us up some o' that horsemeat, little lady?"

She pinched her mouth in discomfort at the reminder of where the meat had come from, but she said nothing. When the meat was clean she sliced off four steaks.

"Only four?" Waring asked.

"I . . . couldn't. Really." She grimaced even as she handled the meat.

"Ah, she'll be all right, Johnny," Fyle said

with a laugh. "Does she get hungry enough she'll jus' jump right in there. Why, it's positively amazin' what a body will do to keep hisself in one piece." He gave a furry little laugh from deep in his throat. Veach got the impression that Fyle's amusement had nothing to do with Ann Waring's reluctance to eat horsemeat. The man seemed to be thinking of something else entirely.

Ann Waring removed the rocks from the surface of her stove and arranged them under the injured man's blankets before she put a large skillet onto the stove. The unconscious man did not stir when his covering was disturbed.

Waring tucked the blankets close around the man's neck, then stoked the stove firebox to build the heat up to a level suitable for frying. His wife gingerly placed the four steaks into the skillet and poked at them with a fork until they were positioned to satisfy her. Fyle observed the movements of both people without offering to help. Bo Jim Hatch seemed lost in a distant and very private place of retreat.

The meat was little different from fresh beef — slightly darker, slightly more coarsely grained, perhaps slightly sweeter in flavor as well. Veach could not decide if the differences were real or imagined. Which-

239

ever, the differences were not so great as to interfere with the satisfaction that came from having a hot, solid meal of red meat. It was the first meal they had had in several days that required a decent amount of cutting and chewing, and he felt better for it — and warmer as well.

There were still three mules and four horses grazing somewhere nearby, he realized. Viewed as a source of food, those animals made their situation seem far less dangerous. Veach cocked an eye at Jimbo Fyle, whose fingers and skin were greasy with meat juices. The man was contentedly stuffing the last of his steak into his mouth. Fyle had seen the livestock as a walking commissary all along, Veach suddenly thought. That would certainly account for his lack of concern over their supply of food. As for how many of the animals might have to be slaughtered before the weather broke, Veach was equally certain that Fyle would not really care as long as enough remained to transport two men out with the thaw. Jimbo returned his glance and winked. Had anyone asked, Veach would have sworn the man knew what he had been thinking at that moment. It made Veach distinctly uncomfortable. He lowered his eyes and concentrated on the rest of his meat.

CHAPTER 21

"Here now, Veach. Whyn't you move over by the stove t'night, hey? You been out in the cold, boy. It'll be warmer here. Ol' Jimbo don't mind. I'll bunk down in your regular spot." Fyle was smiling broadly, ingratiating and pleasant.

Veach's reaction was suspicious caution at the unexpected offer. Fyle had not shown any consideration for another person previously, and Veach immediately wondered why he would do so now.

"What a kind thing for you to suggest, Mr. Fyle," the woman said in a bright and cheerful tone.

Veach looked at her and for a moment felt ashamed of his own unvoiced reaction. Mrs. Waring was undoubtedly right, he decided. Fyle's offer might be a bit late, but it *was* thoughtful. And Veach certainly was uncomfortably cold again after venturing outside with the other men while the woman had her few minutes of privacy. Veach swallowed his suspicions and by way of atonement offered his hand to Jimbo Fyle. "I'm grateful to you, Jimbo, and I'll take you up on that offer if you will accept a thank-you."

"Ah sure, you don't need t' be thanking me. Me an' Bo Jim always try t' do the decent thing, see." Fyle chuckled to himself and turned to unroll his blankets beside the bunk. Veach spread his next to the stove.

With both spare blankets piled atop the injured man there was no longer a curtain dividing the cabin. If Ann Waring had had the comfort and the normality of a nightdress before — and Veach was not sure whether she had — she would not any longer. Veach had imagined before how attractive she must be in sleep. Now he would know. And so would the others. He tried to put it out of his mind.

"What about him?" Veach asked with a gesture toward the sleeping stranger.

John Waring pulled at his chin. "I have given it some thought," he admitted. "I believe he will be better off to remain in the bunk where he has been."

"But . . . you and Mrs. Waring . . . ?"

"Will be there too. It will be crowded, but I see no alternative."

"Ah, no need for that, Johnny. Why, hell,

there's scarce room for you an' the little lady as it is. You jus' lay that fella down alongside o' me, you hear?" Jimbo offered. "Leave my blankets for a ground cloth, you see, an' lay them extras atop. An' my heat will help keep him warm. Be just fine like that. Just fine." He smiled and knelt to smooth his blankets on the hard earth floor.

"I must say, Fyle, that is awfully generous of you."

"No, John."

Waring turned to look at his wife. "Why, Ann? It sounds like a good idea to me."

She hesitated, and Veach got the impression that the woman did not fully know why she disliked the suggestion; she knew only that she did. She said, "I don't think he should be disturbed that much, John. And you know the floor is too cold for a man in his condition." She took her husband by the arm and turned him back toward the bunk. "Just move him to the edge, John. I can crawl back by the wall, and you can slip in between us. There should be room enough." She giggled. "Barely."

"Ah now, Johnny, I don't see no need for you folks t' be uncomfortable the whole night through. Put him down by me, I say. He's gonna die anyhow. Won't make no difference to him either way."

Waring gave him a cold look. "I wish you'd quit saying he will die, Fyle. He seems to be doing quite well, considering. And if Ann wants him to remain where he is, then, sir, we will leave him undisturbed."

Fyle nodded pleasantly. "Whatever you folks want, Johnny. Just tryin' to be helpful, I was."

"Yes . . . well . . . we appreciate your co-operation, but we will decline. Thank you just the same."

"Oh sure, Johnny. Don't think nothing of it." Fyle nodded politely to each of them and slipped beneath his blankets. He laid his hat aside and settled himself for the night.

Bo Jim Hatch was also in his blankets and ready for sleep, Veach saw. "I'll get the lamp after you're settled," Veach offered.

"We won't be a moment," Waring said.

Veach turned his back to give them at least that much privacy. He opened the firebox door and dropped in a few of the largest wood chunks they had on hand, knowing they would not last through the night. He wondered if he could will himself to waken every few hours so he could maintain the cabin's warmth. He did not know if he could do that, but he decided to try. If it worked it would be more comfortable for all of them, especially for the injured man.

When Veach turned back the Warings were in bed. At the near edge of the narrow bunk the unconscious visitor was a pasty, slack-jawed face above a dark background of mounded blankets. Veach was careful not to look beyond to the gold blur of Ann Waring's hair. Her husband, squeezed in the middle, was peering wide-eyed past the injured man's head. Veach gave him a brief nod and leaned forward to blow the lamp out.

The floor was no softer beside the stove, the protruding stones no fewer, but it was certainly warmer. Veach stretched and yawned, luxuriating in the welcome and now much-appreciated comfort of being both warm and fed. Outside, the temperature was still below zero as closely as they could judge, but at least for this moment he was content.

Inside one of the burning wood chunks a few feet from Veach's ear a pocket of moisture thawed and steamed into hissing life until the expanding vapor became too much for the wood fibers to contain. It snapped aloud in a miniature explosion. Veach sighed his approval of the sound and nestled deeper into his folded blankets. Free from worry for the time being, he let himself sink pleasurably into sleep.

He wakened some time later, aware that he had slept, aware somehow of the passage of time, but unable to know when the transition had been made from wakefulness to sleep and back again. Veach blinked his eyes and enjoyed the blanket-held pocket of warmth that surrounded him. He shifted one foot experimentally to the side and discovered the heavy woolen cloth of his blankets not yet too cold. He could afford to wait a few minutes and enjoy the period of leisure before he fed more wood into the stove.

On the other side of the table and chairs Jimbo Fyle sat upright on the floor, his blankets falling to his waist. He moved without previous stirring or shifting, as if he had lain awake while the others slept.

Veach, unwilling to disturb his comfort and not especially anxious to speak to Jimbo Fyle, heard the falling cloth but remained silent. He turned his head toward Fyle, although there was little he could see: only the faintest amount of light escaped from the firebox, and two of the table legs were between them. He could barely make out the different degrees of darkness of Jimbo's seated form.

The man seemed to turn slightly and to

reach toward the Warings' bunk. He would have been sitting immediately beside the injured man, Veach remembered. He decided Fyle must have been checking the man's condition. That was a good thing, Veach decided, because now that he thought about it he realized that he could hear harsh, labored breathing coming from the bunk.

Satisfied that everything was under control, Veach drowsed again. Several hours later he wakened and fed the fire, careful to make as little noise as possible. He was pleased when he realized that all the breathing he could hear in the single room was deep and regular and even. He lay back down and snuggled into his blankets.

"Veach! Wake up, man."

He groaned, reluctant to leave the comfort of his sleep, but someone was gripping his shoulder and shaking him. The voice kept repeating his name, softly but insistently. He opened his eyes.

John Waring was bending over him. Someone had lighted the lamp, but had turned it so low that the flame was no more than a single candle would have produced. Waring's face was in shadow.

Veach sat and shook the sleep from his

head. "Wha . . . ?"

"Shush," Waring hissed. In a whisper he said, "Ann is still asleep. I . . . hate to disturb you. Wouldn't need to, really, but we need to build the fire up before we, uh, open the door."

"What's going on?"

"That man. He died during the night. I guess Fyle was right after all. In any event I don't want Ann to see him now. He is, well, quite blue in the face. Not at all an attractive sight. Fyle said he and Hatch will take the, uh, body outside. So would you mind?"

"Mind? Mind what?"

"Moving. That's why I wakened you. You're in the way, you see."

"Oh. Yeah." Veach rubbed his eyes and mumbled a few curses, careful to keep the sounds low enough so that the woman could not have heard even if she had been awake. Again he shook his head in an effort to clear his thoughts. "Look, I'll get the stove going. I'm awake now. Really."

Waring straightened and stepped back. "All right."

Veach looked around the dimly lighted cabin. Fyle was sitting at the table, his coat already on and his gloves on the table surface before him. Bo Jim was in his usual position beside the door. Little light reached him there. A dot of yellow lamplight was reflected in his unmoving eyes. Waring stood looking nervously toward the bunk, which held both his sleeping wife and a dead stranger.

Guarding carefully against clattering the door latch, Veach eased the firebox open and used a slim billet of split wood to stir the night's accumulation of ashes down through the grate. By the time he had done that his wooden poker had caught fire at the tip, ignited by embers that had remained alive within a coating of ash. He shoved the burning prod the rest of the way into the stove and began adding more and larger pieces. The wood was dry and quickly produced a noisy flame that filled the firebox and began radiating heat into the cabin.

Jimbo beckoned Hatch to him and the two of them easily plucked the dead man from the bunk edge. The body appeared to be no burden at all to them, although Veach remembered quite well how heavy the man had been when he and Waring brought him inside.

"Careful you don't bump the chair," Waring whispered. "I'll get the door for you."

A tangle of blanket was draped across the man's stomach and trailing onto the floor. Veach stepped forward to lift it away. Clad only in woolen underwear, the dead man looked quite small. It occurred to Veach that none of them knew so much as how tall the man had been. None of them had ever seen him on his feet.

Fyle had his upper body, lifting him by his arms. The man's head lolled back, his head and a lank fall of light brown hair swaying rhythmically from side to side as Fyle shuffled forward. As Waring had said, his flesh was unnaturally dark, his cheeks mottled and lips purplish. He looked even thinner, more gaunt than Veach remembered. With his head dropped at such an angle his throat presented a knife-edge sharpness with the flesh sunken and pulled away from it. Veach noticed a curious break in the line of his throat, a dark depression marring the line of cartilage there.

Waring lifted the latch and eased the door open, and Fyle and Hatch carried the body out into the frigid air. Waring shut the door behind them. "Well, I guess that is that. We certainly tried, though. We did everything we could."

"You did, John, you and Ann both . . ." Veach's eyes narrowed. "Oh *hell,* John. I just realized. Did you see that boy's throat? And his face? Think about it, John. I think maybe he didn't just die. I think maybe he was killed. Somebody could've taken hold of his throat and just pinched. In his condition a squeeze with two fingers would have killed him."

"Come on now, Veach." Waring's voice was puzzled, disbelieving. "We tried to *save* him. No one would have any reason to harm him. Why, I was the only one next to him. I slept beside him the night through. Surely you aren't accusing me . . ."

Veach shook his head impatiently, angrily. "Dammit, John. Listen to me. I woke up once during the night. I saw Jimbo reach up to him. Fyle was right beside him too, you know. At the time I thought Fyle was checking to see was he all right. Why, he could have been murdering that poor fellow while I watched, and me not even knowing it."

"That's an awfully serious accusation, Veach."

"Damn right it is. Serious as they come, mister."

"Why then? Why would Fyle want to harm a man who couldn't possibly hurt him? That makes no sense."

"I don't know why, John. I just believe it's so, that's all. Why, dammit, I believe I saw a man murdered right here in this cabin."

"Keep your voice down, please," Waring hissed.

"I'm sorry," Veach said more quietly. "But, John, I swear I believe I'm right about that."

Waring shook his head. "I simply can't agree. Fyle would have no reason to do such a thing. Why, he said all along the boy would die from his exposure to the cold. Even if he had a reason to wish the man dead, why would he kill a dying man?"

"I don't *know,* dammit," Veach said helplessly. "Maybe he decided we were right. Maybe he saw that your missus was going to pull the boy out of it. How would I know what would make him do it? I just say he did it."

Waring started to reply, but the sound of the door latch being opened cut his words short. Both Veach and Waring were standing, silently staring at one another, when Jimbo Fyle and Bo Jim Hatch shouldered their way back into the warmth of the cabin. Fyle stamped the snow from his boots and grinned at them. "Well now, boys, I guess that's tended to."

CHAPTER 22

Ann Waring seemed badly shaken by the man's death. Her own youth and a sheltered, highly protected background had left her as yet unfamiliar with the subject in any but the most abstract terms. In her previous experience dead would have been a word rather than a condition. Sleeping in the same bed with a dead body left her visibly shaken, possibly on the verge of hysteria.

Waring comforted her as well as he could. Had they been alone he might have held her and petted her fears away and could have encouraged her flow of tears. As it was, with strangers present where they could not avoid hearing and seeing his ministrations to his wife, John Waring displayed an awkward, embarrassed reluctance to give her the reassuring physical contact she needed. The most he could do was to sit beside her, holding her hand and grieving for her.

Veach was aware of the acute discomfort

being shared by the Warings, but he could see neither sympathy nor even awareness in the others. Jimbo Fyle sat at the table, making no effort to conceal his impatience for his breakfast. Bo Jim Hatch sat cross-legged by the door, openly watching Ann Waring's emotions shift and flow in her facial expressions.

Embarrassed for the Warings, Veach looked around the cabin seeking something, any sort of busywork, that would hold his attention away from them. In the front corner of the cabin, lying beside Ann Waring's piled trunks, he saw the tangle of clothing they had stripped from the dead man when they brought him inside the previous day. Veach gathered them up and carried them to the table. He sat with his back to the Warings and arranged the clothes across his lap.

"An' what would you be doin' with those now?" Fyle asked. "Taken to robbing the dead, have you?"

Veach gave the man a look of disgust. "We don't even know his name, you know. I thought there might be something in here to tell us. We could carve a marker maybe. Do something, anyhow."

Fyle snorted. "You figure to bury him, do you? Hell. It'd take a hill of powder to open a grave in this kinda weather. An' even then it'd wash out come spring. Just let him lay, I say. Me an' Bo Jim put him on that pile o' stuff beside the cabin. Cold as it is he won't putrefy there. Not 'til we're long gone, he won't."

"I don't intend to dig any graves right now," Veach said, willing into his voice a patience he did not feel. "I'd just like to know. All right?"

Fyle sat back and gave him a palm-lifted gesture and an expression of wounded innocence. "Sure now. Just trying to be helpful, I was."

Veach bent his head and ignored Fyle. The dead man's coat was a good one, made of well-tanned leather and blanket-lined for extra warmth. It was far better made and far heavier than Veach's coat. It also looked like it would fit him. He decided he would try it on later. Its owner had no further need of it. He thought fleetingly of Fyle's jibe about robbing the dead and did his best to ignore it.

One pocket of the coat held a flat tin box with a tightly fitted sliding cover. The box contained eight sulphur-tipped matches and a strip of sand-coated board for a striking surface. The other pocket was empty. Veach set the box of matches on the table and dropped the coat onto the floor beside his chair.

"He was a city fellow, whoever he was," Veach observed aloud.

"Why'd you say that?" Fyle asked.

Veach pulled his hand out of the man's right-hand trouser pocket. A ring holding four keys dangled from one finger. "Not many locks on a pick or a saddle," he said. He dropped the keys beside the tin box.

From the same pocket he withdrew a slim, two-bladed folding knife far smaller than the clasp or belt knives that would be found on anyone used to traveling in rough country. Fyle plucked the little knife from his fingers and pulled open the larger blade. He tested it against the ball of his thumb and made a face. "A finger-nail'd be sharper," he said.

In the other pants pocket Veach found twenty-seven cents in coin and a brass medallion with a picture of a bearded man on one side. Veach did not recognize the figure.

"If that was a good-luck piece it did a helluva lousy job," Fyle said. He took it from the tabletop where Veach had laid it and spun it into the air. The metal disk flashed in the lamplight and made a tinny, whirring sound until it smacked loudly onto

Fyle's cupped palm. Veach dropped the trousers onto the floor and picked up the dead man's shirt.

"John." He turned toward the Warings, barely able to keep himself from smiling at what he had found. A tobacco pouch tag dangled from the shirt pocket.

Veach took the pouch from the pocket and did smile. The cloth sack was nearly full and had three books of papers tucked behind the paper wrapper.

Waring nodded. "Go ahead if you like, Veach. I'll load my pipe after we eat."

"When's that gonna be, anyhow?" Fyle grumbled.

Waring sighed. "Soon, Mr. Fyle. It won't be long now. My wife needs a few moments more to . . . compose herself."

Fyle grunted.

Eagerly Veach pulled a paper from one of the folders, creased it and spilled a pinch of the loose tobacco onto the paper. He shaped and moistened the cigarette and used one of the dead man's matches to light it rather than going to the stove. He drew the smoke deep into his lungs and involuntarily coughed. After a full day without a smoke it tasted dry and unpleasant. Veach smiled broadly. "Wonderful," he said.

Fyle shook his head in disgust. "Damn

shame the boy wasn't carrying something useful, like liquor."

"This will do just fine for me," Veach said. He drew in another lungful of smoke and exhaled past teeth that were exposed in a grin. He flipped the spent match stem toward the woodbox and watched it bounce instead to the floor.

Feeling almost content now, Veach picked up the shirt with the intention of dropping it onto the other clothing beside his chair. His fingers encountered another solid object inside the shirt pocket, which he had thought he had emptied. Veach cocked his head and squinted one eye shut against the welcome sting of smoke rising from the end of his cigarette. With two fingers he dipped again into the shirt pocket.

"What've we got here?" he muttered aloud.

At first he thought it was a good-luck medallion and was about to comment on the number of them the man had carried. Instead it turned out to be a nickeled disk the size of a silver dollar with a star and the words "Special Deputy" engraved on the surface. A pin clasp on the back of the badge had been broken. Veach glanced once at Jimbo Fyle before he reached around to hand the article to John Waring. For a few minutes he had forgotten his suspicions about Fyle. Now they came flooding back.

Waring examined the small badge, turning it over in his hands but unable to gain more information from it by staring.

"What is it, dear?" It was the first interest Ann Waring had shown in anything since they had told her about her patient's death.

Waring told her.

She brightened somewhat, her face losing the blank, drawn emptiness of in-turned anguish and taking on some animation again. "You mean he was a policeman then?"

"Not a regular one," Veach responded. "A full-time deputy would have a regular sort of badge. Something fancier than this. This is the sort of thing they'd give to a fellow riding as a sworn member of a posse or something like that. Something temporary."

Jimbo Fyle snorted and waved his hand. "Ah, that don't mean nothing, a little scrap of metal. Why there's lots of boys runnin' beef in these big counties that carries them little badges so they got an excuse to shoot any hungry traveler that needs some meat to feed his family. That's prob'ly what this fella was. A cowboy with one of them badges in his pocket all the time."

Veach shook his head. "That wasn't any

cowboy," he reasoned. "Not carrying a ring of keys and a little penknife like that. No, he was definitely from some town somewhere. He was more than likely sworn into a posse and came out this far for some good reason. Probably from over on the Idaho side, since he didn't come up from the east. Maybe following some criminals trying to get from one territory into another."

Fyle laughed easily. "You sure got it all figured, don't you? Think you do anyhow, eh? Well I'll tell you somethin' else. Even if you're right it don't matter to him now. He's dead now an' so is everybody else that was with him. Froze an' stiff an' no threat to nobody now, they ain't."

"Why, Mr. Fyle," the woman protested, "you sound almost pleased about that. That poor young man is dead and you say others may have died also. I would think you might express some concern for them. To say nothing about concern for the capture of anyone they may have been chasing."

Jimbo Fyle's good humor disappeared abruptly. "I got concern enough, by God, without bein' told what I ought by some damned woman." He glared at Waring. "She's had enough pampering now. It's about time we eat."

Waring was halfway off the bunk when

Veach stiff-armed him back into a sitting position. "Calm down now. Everybody. Just settle down," Veach said.

Frustrated, Waring muttered a coarse epithet to the room at large. Fyle thought it was directed at him. He bolted from his chair and tried to charge around the table that was between him and Waring. The point of his hip banged into the table and sent it smashing into Veach's side.

Veach nearly fell, but caught himself and spun to intercept Fyle. Both he and Ann Waring jumped in front of Jimbo as the burly man rounded the end of the table.

Fyle was angry, but coldly so. Far from being red-faced in his anger, the man's face was drained of color. He was in full control of himself, for he made no effort to overpower the man and the woman blocking his way, although he could have done so with ease. His eyes were narrowed and, Veach thought, quite coldly cruel. Veach had had little doubt before that Jimbo Fyle killed the injured deputy. Now, seeing him like this, he had none at all.

"John wasn't talking to you," the woman was saying. "He *wasn't.* Really. He truly wasn't, Mr. Fyle." In her anxiety her words tumbled together until it sounded as if she was babbling incoherently, although her intent was to calm and to soothe Fyle.

His cold-eyed stare left John Waring and dropped to the woman who was clinging so desperately to his left arm. He had to lean backward to gain enough distance that he could see her clearly. "Shut up." The voice was as cold as the look in his eyes. She did. His gaze returned slowly to John Waring. Waring returned the look in full measure.

Waring unfolded himself from his seat on the bunk edge. He drew himself to his full height and stood stiffly erect. "The word was not directed at you," Waring said. His chin rose in quiet defiance. "Perhaps it should have been. I will no longer tolerate your rudeness to my wife, nor your vulgarity in her presence. Do you understand this, sir?"

Fyle's eyes narrowed. His expression was washed with contempt. "You ain't being so prudent right now, Johnny." The absence of any heat of anger from tone and word seemed to Veach more menacing than any explosive outburst could have been.

"Prudence only goes so far, Fyle."

The larger man grunted. He looked for a moment toward Bo Jim Hatch, who sat unmoving but attentive beside the door. Fyle seemed to be thinking through some extended train of thought. After a moment he nodded as if to himself. He shook himself free from the ineffectual restraint imposed by Veach and the woman. He turned and moved with tight, catlike grace back to his overturned chair. He bent to resettle the chair onto four legs and flowed smoothly into a relaxed and normal position at the table. "Will you ask your woman to fix a meal, Waring?" he asked in a tone that to all outward indications was calm and even cordial.

John Waring sucked in a long breath, held it for a moment and let it out softly. He nodded. "I will."

"It will be ready in just a minute, John," she promised quickly. She got busy at the stove, and Veach returned to his chair.

Bo Jim Hatch lumbered to his feet. He looked at each of them in turn, his concentration for a few seconds given wholly to first one and then another of the occupants of the small cabin, but his expression was too veiled to give any hint of what he might have been thinking. Hatch pulled on his heavy garments, picked up the water bucket and left.

CHAPTER 23

As soon as the water bucket was full and Ann Waring had everything she needed to prepare their meal, the four men filed out into the deep cold to give the woman a few minutes of privacy. No fresh snow had fallen, but neither had the cold abated. The snow cover around the cabin was much trampled now, churned and rumpled and far from the deceptively eye-appealing ground cover it had been. Veach was wearing the lined coat that had belonged to the dead man, and he felt much more comfortable in it in spite of its former ownership.

Waring had given up on trying to preserve the remaining forage by penning his mules at night, so there was no longer any need for him to go to the shelter. Still, by habit that now seemed firmly established, Waring and Veach turned toward the livestock shed while Fyle and Hatch separated from them and turned downstream toward the pile of boulders. Veach glanced nervously over his shoulder at the receding backs of the other two men, but Waring ignored them.

When they were safely out of the other men's hearing Veach said, "I'm more sure of it than ever, Waring. Do you believe me now? Do you think Jimbo Fyle might've killed that boy?"

"I'd consider it a possibility," Waring said calmly. "There would also be the possibility that we might be in danger too, you know."

"Don't I know it." Veach drew in a deep breath, held it for a moment and exhaled slowly. He tugged his hat down tighter and said, "That's a dangerous pair, John, and I think your woman is in more danger from them than we are, if you know what I mean. The way Fyle was looking at her this morning and the way Bo Jim was talking yesterday, well . . ."

Waring's eyebrows lifted in inquiry.

"That's right," Veach said. "I started out to tell you about that yesterday morning and then you spotted that deputy lying in the snow. I never got back to thinking about it, I guess." Veach told him what Hatch had so casually said about liking Ann Waring . . . and that a husband was of no consequence in the matter if he could not physically defend his woman from Bo Jim.

"Between that and the way Fyle was this morning, well, I think we have troubles here," Veach said. He sighed. "I swear I'd feel a lot better if I had a gun. I never especially wanted to wear one before, but now I wish I did. You wouldn't have a spare, would you?"

Waring laughed. "A spare? The only thing I have here is a rifle, and a single-shot Sharps at that. It's in the corner beside Ann's trunks." He pulled at his chin thoughtfully. "At least it is out of sight there."

"Loaded?"

He shook his head. "Not in the house."

"That's kind of a shame, you know. Whatever happened to the deputy's gun? I hadn't thought before, but he had one on his belt when we carried him inside."

"If I remember correctly I put it at the foot of the bed along with his clothing."

"It isn't there now."

"No, it certainly isn't. I, uh, assume Fyle did us the favor of putting it away for us."

"It would be somewhere in their gear then, John. We could go back in. Find it. Have that and your rifle ready when they come in."

"What you are suggesting, Veach, is the same as murder."

"No, sir. What I am suggesting is that we defend ourselves — and your missus — from someone who already committed a murder right there in your cabin. Mister, I just don't want to be the next one to go under, and that's a fact."

Deep-seated pain showed behind John Waring's eyes. "I cannot believe that that would be necessary, Mr. Veach. But perhaps we might . . . disarm them . . . just to protect ourselves."

"And keep the two of them under guard around the clock until the weather breaks? No, John. No way. It could be weeks before we get a chinook blowing through here. The least little slackening of attention and they'd get us for sure. We either cut down on them by surprise or we wait for them to decide what *they* are going to do and when they want to do it. We don't have any other choices."

"Oh, Lord," John Waring whispered. It was not a casual exclamation. It was a prayer of appeal. He hunkered in the boot-packed snow beside the shed and stared at the ground. When he looked up at Veach his expression was filled with regret. "I am not a murderer," he said. "I cannot shoot an unsuspecting man."

Veach cursed softly, but without rancor in

267

his tone. "I think you're wrong, John. I think we're both wrong. But I'm kinda glad that's what you decided. I guess I mostly feel that way myself, though I could do it otherwise if you agreed. I still think it would be the safest thing for us to do, but . . ."

They heard the cabin door slam and a brief, startled yelp that was Ann Waring's voice. Both men began running toward the cabin.

"Shut the door, boys," Jimbo said pleasantly. He was seated at the table with his legs crossed, still wearing his parka. He held his big revolver loosely in his right hand, aiming it nowhere in particular but intimidating them with its presence.

Bo Jim was seated on the edge of the Warings' bunk. He was smiling, more life and animation in his face than they had seen there before. Ann Waring was in the bunk beside him, slumped into the back corner of the cabin. She looked frightened and very small. Bo Jim held her wrist in his huge left hand. His right held a revolver that seemed to be a twin of his partner's.

"I said close the door, boys. You're lettin' the cold in."

Veach pushed the door to and watched the latch drop into place. It reminded him somehow of Bo Jim's slow, studied thoroughness with minor tasks. The back of Veach's neck crawled at the thought of Bo Jim Hatch and Fyle behind him. He wanted to snatch the door open and bolt outside. It was neither the cold outside nor the vulnerability of the Warings if left alone in the cabin that kept him from running. Rather it was the memory of the revolver in Jimbo Fyle's hand and a firm belief that the man could and would use the gun at the least provocation. He turned back to face the single room.

"That's better, boys. No point to everybody gettin' cold, is there?" Jimbo said conversationally. He seemed completely at ease, completely in control of the situation. Defiance of his will seemed — to him and to the others — beyond the possible.

John Waring looked carefully around the room. He seemed to be assessing people, objects, distances from one to the other. Veach hoped Waring was able to find a magic key that would free them from this predicament; he himself could see none, nor any hope of one. Apparently Waring could not either. The man shrugged his shoulders and walked to the table. He seated himself opposite Jimbo Fyle and asked, "Now what?"

Jimbo grinned and waved the muzzle of his revolver toward the bunk. "Ol' Bo Jim was kinda peeved with me just now 'cause I was still tellin' him he couldn't take your woman, Johnny. He kinda went off to sulk, you see, an' he come back with something almighty interesting." The grin faded and his expression hardened, turned colder.

"It struck me as awful unfriendly, Johnny," he said, "when I was tryin' to do right by you folks. I mean, boy, I was really tryin' to be nice to you. I never *had* to keep ol' Bo Jim offa your woman, now did I? But I done that, all right. I figured we could hole up here an' be decent t' one another an' when the weather broke me an' Bo Jim could ride off an' leave you people be. An' what happens when I try to be nice? What does Bo Jim find?" He dug his left hand deep into a pocket and brought out a grayish lump of slag. "I've seen the like o' this before, Johnny. You been meltin' gold here, Johnny. You got yourself a poke put by somewhere here or close by." His voice took on a steely edge.

"You figure you've got it all, don't you, Johnny? All to yourself. Sack o'gold. Fine-lookin' woman. All to yourself. Never a thought for helpin' those as needs it, either, Johnny. You wasn't even gonna feed us when we come in here cold an' hungry. Had to fetch our own supplies in or we wasn't welcome. An' Bo Jim had t' go out in the cold t' fetch that meat back. *You* never stirred your butt outta this cabin. All the while tryin' to hide from us that you're a rich man. An' us just a couple poor old boys. Well, Johnny, now we *do* know 'bout it, you see. Now the question is, are we gonna leave *you* anything when we go, not th' other way round." Fyle shook his head in mock sadness. "I jus' don't know, Johnny."

"I suppose it is a silly question, Fyle, but just what is it that you want of us?"

Jimbo barked out a short, ugly laugh. "Silly as hell, Johnny. We want you should hand over your poke, of course."

Waring sighed. He sat back in his chair and let his chin sink toward his chest while he thought. Finally he said, "You put us all in a very bad situation here, Fyle. I would gladly give you the entire amount if it would mean we would be left in peace afterward. Unfortunately I see no way I could trust you to give, uh, acceptable assurances that this would be so."

"Ah now, Johnny. You see there? Do you? You're sayin' you don't want to take Jimbo's word. That's what you're sayin', Johnny.

An' after I've tried so hard to trust you an' treat you decent. That don't seem right, Johnny. It don't for a fact now."

"Look at it from our point of view, Fyle. You are in the process of robbing us, and neither party has anywhere to go once the robbery is completed. Until the chinook comes we must all remain here, regardless of what else happens."

"Ah now, Johnny, maybe that ain't so at all. Maybe me an' Bo Jim would jus' run you boys outside an' turn you loose after we have your poke. Maybe I could give you Jimbo Fyle's word on that, Johnny. My word's good, Johnny. It surely is. Jimbo Fyle don't have to lie to no man."

"We would die in the cold as surely as the posse that youngster was with." Waring tilted his head up and squinted thoughtfully at Fyle. "They were after you two, weren't they? That's why you killed that boy, of course."

Jimbo snorted. He sounded proud of himself. "Figured that out, did you? Hell, it seemed better'n causing a fuss should the little whelp live. An' he had to be the last o' that bunch. The cold took care of the rest of 'em for us."

"How many were there, Fyle?"

"Eight of them, wasn't there, Bo?"

272

The larger man released his hold on Ann Waring's wrist, allowing her to edge back more deeply into the corner. His expression showed deep concentration and his lips moved soundlessly as he began to tick off a remembered accounting on his fingers. At length he nodded and agreed, "Eight."

"It must have been a serious crime," Waring said, "for them to send so many on such a long chase."

"Ah, not so much," Fyle said. "They never expected it t' get as serious as it done. They was just havin' fun chasin' us more'n anything else. We robbed us a li'l old store over in Idaho. Didn't get but forty-two dollars, we didn't. Had t' throw a few shots into a crowd. Don't know if we hit anyone real good, though. That's one thing about grab-and-run, see. You never rightly know what you've left behind, but mostly they don't stay on us past when the sport of it runs out an' it gets to bein' hard work or they go to bein' hungry." He grinned. "That's one o' the biggest things right there. Mostly a posse don't take time t' load food an' coffee an' pans, so they don't stay on us long. Me an' Bo Jim, of course, is ready t' run afore we ever start. We know what we're about, all right. Nobody never gives us real trouble. You won't neither, Johnny."

"Do you really believe you can just take whatever we have and then leave?"

Jimbo's grin grew wider. "No, now, Johnny. I been kinda thinking on that since you went an' mentioned it. No, I figure me an' Bo Jim can take whatever you got, Johnny, an' then *you* can leave."

Veach stood beside the door and shivered. On the other side of that slab of wood was a deep and deadly silence from the relentlessly impersonal cold that already might have killed seven men.

Chapter 24

John Waring fingered his chin. "We seem to have something of a stalemate here."

"A stalemate, Johnny? That's kinda like a Mexican standoff, ain't it? Well now, Johnny, I don't know as I can agree with you, m' boy. The way I see it, me an' Bo Jim got all the marbles. You got nothin' we can't have for the taking."

The man seemed to be entirely correct, but Waring smiled a bluff across the table at him. "You have us, Fyle. We have the gold. Perhaps we could find some way to effect a trade."

Jimbo smiled back at him. "Ah, Johnny boy. You already tol' me there's no way you could trust me once I have what I want. An' of course there ain't. Once I got your money an' your woman, I got no use for you at all."

"But you *don't* have that money, Fyle. Nor are you likely to find it without my co-operation. Ann doesn't know where it is, and I might prove quite stubborn about telling you where to find it. In fact, I have little stamina and less courage. If you try to force the information from me I might well die under rough handling. Then no one would ever find it."

Fyle laughed. "You do keep tryin', Johnny. Sure an' you do. But I'll just bet you'll be real willin' to tell me so as to keep your pretty li'l missus from coming to harm, eh?"

John Waring shook his head. "We are back to your standoff, Fyle, squarely on the horns of a dilemma. Of course I would do anything to prevent harm from reaching my wife. But unless I have assurances that my co-operation will genuinely benefit her, my best course of action on her behalf must be to keep my silence."

Fyle scratched himself and looked thoughtful. "Johnny," he drawled, "I kinda believe you'll be real helpful when you've had a chance t' think about me makin' a present of that little lady there t' my pal Bo Jim." He hooked a thumb toward the corner. Ann Waring sat woodenly, eyes dulled by unthinkable thoughts. Hatch again held her wrist clamped in one hand. She might as well have been tethered with locks and chains.

Waring's face went white, a reaction that

was closely observed by Jimbo Fyle.

"Excuse me a minute, fellows." Veach cleared his throat and took a step forward. "There's something you should be thinking about, Jimbo. And you too, Bo Jim." He shoved his hands into his pockets and moved up to the table. The cabin seemed uncomfortably warm now, and he unbuttoned his coat.

"I reckon we know what side you're on in this," Jimbo said.

"Uh-huh. I guess you do. Still, there's something you maybe should think about, Fyle."

Fyle raised an eyebrow in silent inquiry.

"You've been in this country quite a while. Well, I've been out here a couple years myself, Jimbo. Long enough to know how decent folks regard men like you and Bo Jim. Oh, you boys know what you're about, all right. You hit a store or a miner. Rob a freighter. Maybe even a coach or something. You know when you can shoot and know how far you can push folks so they'll chase you — but not too awful hard. You want them to make that run at you and then leave you be. You said as much yourself, talking about that posse that was on you before the snow and the cold hit. You know you will be chased. But only so much.

"Boys, in the past I'd bet you've made many a small hit and thrown shots at people from time to time doing it. No doubt you've shot people before, maybe killed some of them. Well, you can get away with that all right. You know it, and we know it. You could shoot me and you could shoot John Waring, and it'd be a real regrettable thing. Anybody that learned of it would say it was a damned shame. And they'd pretty much let it go at that.

"But, boys, you know as well as I do that if you harm a decent woman like Ann Waring you've the same as put a rope around your own necks. You wouldn't be running from jail then, you'd be running from a hanging. There wouldn't be any posse to outrun. What there'd be would be talk, boys, and you can't outrun that. Anywhere you went somebody would hear or someone else would remember. They'd hate you. Want to get rid of you. You heard what happened to that pair over in Nebraska?" Fyle's eyes flickered uneasily. "That's the kind of treatment you could expect, boys."

"That story is a load of bull anyway, fella," Fyle grumbled without believing his own words.

"No it isn't, Jimbo," Veach pressed. "I hired a mule skinner this past spring who was working in that country when it happened. He said he was there when they brought those bodies into town. Hell, you've seen the picture postcards showing them. 'Most everybody has seen them. Think about that, Jimbo. *Those* boys got themselves unpopular, just like you and Bo Jim will if you harm a woman. The boys that caught up to those two didn't just hang them, Jimbo. Didn't just shoot them. No, they wanted more than that. They strung those boys up slow. No drop to break their necks and make it quick. They pulled those boys up real slow so they'd strangle and turn blue and feel the loss of breath. Then they shot into them while they were trying to kick, Jimbo. And *then* they poured coal oil on them and set them afire. Those pictures are enough to make a man puke, Jimbo. Just think what it'd feel like to get that kind of treatment. That *could* happen to you."

Fyle's calm certainty of control melted. His face flushed red with anger and he surged forward. He swept the table away from him, shoving it into Waring and knocking the man off his chair and onto Bo Jim Hatch. In his fury, spurred by fear, Jimbo Fyle struck out blindly at Veach, forgetting his gun and trying to smash Veach with sheer physical force.

Veach instinctively ducked underneath Fyle's roundhouse slash with the pistol barrel. Veach darted to the side and brought the toe of his boot up solidly into Fyle's groin. Both Fyle and Bo Jim Hatch grunted at the impact. Fyle doubled over with pain and Bo Jim tried to scramble to his feet, although Waring was still sprawled across him.

Without time to think or to plan Veach reacted before either Fyle or Hatch could recover. He bolted for the doorway and clawed at the latch. The door swung open, and a spray of needle-like splinters exploded into Veach's right ear as one of the men behind him got off a snap shot that struck the door. Veach threw himself forward, hit the snow belly down and began rolling. He scrambled to his feet and ran, desperate to put some solid object between himself and the guns at the cabin.

Habit directed his flight upstream, past the livestock shelter where he and Waring had spent their time outdoors. He ran past the shed and darted behind it. He labored through the deep snow piled at the foot of the gorge wall, unwilling to expose himself on the more open expanse of the floor and the stream bed. Within moments his breathing was harsh and difficult, each indrawn gasp of frigid air ripping into and through his chest. The fear sent him plunging on regardless.

Behind him Jimbo Fyle stood in the doorway trembling with fury. Hatch stood beside him, patient, waiting. John Waring was sprawled on the floor on his side, lying on top of what had been one of the chairs. The other chair was upended against the woodbox. The table had been thrown into the corner where it would have prevented the woman from moving had she tried to get up. She had not moved.

Fyle cursed and turned back to face the interior of the cabin. "Like a damn rabbit goin' to ground," he complained. He took the few strides needed to reach the center of the floor and gave vent to his frustrations by kicking John Waring in the ribs. Waring groaned and flopped onto his back.

Jimbo stood with his head down. He forced his breathing to slow, drawing air deep into his lungs and holding it there a moment before releasing it. When he had control of himself he turned to Bo Jim and said, "Close the door." The cold had already invaded the rock-walled structure. With the door left open the stove seemed to have no more effect than a match flame. Fyle picked the chair up and seated himself by where the table should have been. He stared morosely down at Waring.

Bo Jim pushed the door closed and carefully tested the latch with his fingers. Without waiting to be told he moved behind Fyle to the woodbox and began building up the fire in the stove. Waring sat up cautiously. He winced at a stab of pain in his chest. The kick had broken at least one rib. He was weak and dizzy. Favoring his right side, he crawled to his knees and then onto his bunk. With his left hand he reached across to take his wife's hand and cup it in his own. He closed his eyes.

"What about that other fella?" Hatch asked. "You want me to go after him, Jimbo? He won't be far yet."

Fyle shook his head irritably. "Not yet, dammit. I'll tell you when."

Jimbo Fyle was still angry. He could have shot Hatch when the man began talking.

"He can't be far yet, Jimbo. I could get him. Bring him back if you say to."

"Shut up, will you." His voice was crackling with anger. Bo Jim recoiled and moved a few steps away. Fyle got hold of himself and in a more reasonable tone said, "He can't go nowhere anyhow, Bo. The cold'll

282

get him if you don't. I'll tell you when, hear?"

"Yes, Jimbo." Bo Jim went to the door and sank into his accustomed place. Judging from his expression nothing of interest might have happened in days. He sat patiently, although his eyes were no longer unfocused or vague. Bo Jim sat patiently watching Ann Waring.

CHAPTER 25

Veach's legs gave out. He wobbled forward a few steps more and buckled at the knees, dropping thigh deep into the snow. He gasped and shuddered. He bent forward at the waist, his jaw slack, saliva escaping from his open mouth to drool coldly into the light beard stubble of two days' growth.

Snow packed around his lower legs. From the way the temperature flowed through snow-dampened jeans he might as well have been wearing a suit of underwear carved from ice. His legs began to cramp, and he tried to stagger erect. His knees would not do the work unaided, so he pushed with his hands. The effect of putting bare flesh against the frozen ground felt closer to touching flame than ice. When he brushed the snow from his knuckles he saw that his hands were red and swollen.

He swayed, but forced himself to keep his feet. He groped in his coat pockets to find his gloves and only then realized that his coat was still unbuttoned. Fastening the buttons became a major effort. Feeling was rapidly leaving his fingers. His gasping was neither so rapid nor so deep as it had been, though, and he was beginning to feel a little better.

For the first time since he bolted away from the cabin Veach took a look at his surroundings. His panicked dash had carried him less than a mile upstream from the Waring cabin. From where he now stood he could no longer see the cabin, but a straight-rising thread of smoke marked its location for him.

Several hundred yards toward the far wall he could see the line of footprints, stark against the snow, where the dead man had walked and where he and Bo Jim Hatch had backtrailed him. Veach found it hard to believe that that had been only the previous day. It seemed much longer ago.

At least, he thought, he need not starve. The rest of the dead man's horse would still be upstream from him. Hurriedly he patted his pockets with numbed, glove-bulky hands, checking and checking again to verify his limited sense of touch. He did have his folding knife.

Once he had begun he continued to take

inventory of the few things he now possessed. He carried little in his pockets. Most of what he owned was still back at Waring's. In another pocket he had a bandanna. This he removed and tied over his ears as he had seen others do. It seemed to make little difference in the burning sensation the cold air was causing in his earlobes and it made his hat fit awkwardly, but he left it in place.

Digging a gloved hand into a shirt pocket, he discovered that he still had the dead man's tobacco sack and papers. Far more important, he found that when he had lighted his cigarette earlier he had unthinkingly stuck the man's tin of matches in beside the tobacco. The tin still held seven matches, if he remembered correctly. He thought about taking the box out and opening it to see. He clenched and opened his fists several times and decided to leave the tin alone. If his numbed fingers allowed the matches to spill into the snow the harm would be irreparable. He would not chance it.

For a moment he wished he had a rifle or a handgun to defend himself with. He began to smile then and started chuckling out loud.

As long as you're wishing, he told himself, why not go the whole hog and wish for warm weather and good food and for Jimbo Fyle and Bo Jim Hatch to be swept away to another part of the world. If you are going in for wishing you might as well do a proper job of it. He imagined himself in a brightly lighted, well-heated, high-ceilinged hotel room with a bucket of champagne on one side and a pair of attractive blondes on the other. In his brief mental image, though, both blondes looked like Ann Waring, and he decided he felt no better for having indulged himself in such foolishness.

Besides, if he intended to survive he needed to keep moving. He needed to find a place that would allow him to escape both the cold and the men behind him in the cabin.

As he walked he wondered what had happened — perhaps was happening — to John and Ann Waring. He remembered hearing no shots except the one that had been fired at him as he was running from the cabin. That did not mean the Warings were safe, he knew. For men with the strength of Fyle and Hatch it would probably be as easy to bludgeon or to strangle someone as to shoot them, and it would be far less messy. Both could be dead by now. There was no way he could know, either way.

Regardless, he felt sure that at least one of

the outlaws would come after him. He hoped they would rely on the weather to kill him. He knew he would have a far better chance if they did, perhaps even a good chance. But he knew also that he did not dare count on them remaining warm inside the cabin. Bo Jim especially seemed impervious to the effects of the cold, and it would be very like Fyle to send the huge and relentless Bo Jim after him.

Even if the Warings were dead, Veach decided, Fyle would probably stay inside the cabin himself while Hatch took care of the simple detail of finding and finishing Dan Veach.

Somehow, he decided, he had to prepare himself to face an armed and physically superior hunter. He knew he would need food and, if possible, warmth as well. He began to head purposefully toward the dead horse, his attention on the gorge walls and on the snowfield behind him.

"You want I should go after that fella yet, Jimbo?"

"Did I tell you to shut up, you stupid sonuvabitch? Now shut your mouth or I'll rip *both* your ears off. Leave you worse off than me, b'damn."

Bo Jim subsided. Jimbo *could* tear his ears

off if he wanted to. Bo Jim would not question Jimbo.

Ann Waring's eyes were closed and her breathing seemed normal although she did not look comfortable, slumped as she was against the bare rock of the wall corner.

Waring took one of the blankets shoved untidily at the foot of the bed and carefully smoothed and folded it. Fyle's eyes were on him with every motion. He folded the blanket into a thick pad and put a hand behind Ann's neck to lift her forward a few inches while he tucked the pad behind her back.

She opened her eyes to look at him, but offered neither help nor resistance while he positioned her. He let her back down onto the blanket and received a weak smile of thanks.

She was not an especially strong woman. She certainly was not prepared to cope with a situation such as this. The entire burden of responsibility for her safety would fall on her husband. John Waring seemed worried, unsure if he was capable of meeting her needs now.

At the far side of the table, replaced now where it belonged, Fyle sat brooding. Jimbo could crush John Waring any moment he chose to do so, but if he did he might never find that gold hoard the man had tucked away somewhere. Judging from the slag pile outside there should be hundreds of dollars lying somewhere nearby, and Waring could tell him where it was.

If the woman had known its whereabouts this thing would present no problem — he could just get rid of her husband and ask her where the cache was. He had no doubt that she would tell him. But her man had said she did not know, and Fyle believed him. Not that Waring would not lie to him. Lying was only to be expected, especially by a desperate man. But Jimbo would never trust a woman with knowledge of a secret like the location of a man's poke. He knew better than that. And Waring was no fool either. Jimbo could see plainly enough that John Waring was a smart man and an educated one. So he believed the man when he said he had not told his woman where the poke was.

The problem with that was that there was little he could do to get at the truth now. Except that one thing. That was his key to opening Waring's mouth. Work on the woman a bit and the man would beg him to take his gold. Yet that damned Veach was right, Jimbo admitted to himself. If they molested a woman . . . He shuddered. The thought of a mob turned him cold.

Jimbo trusted no man to keep his mouth shut, either. And, knowing how stupid Bo Jim could be, Jimbo would not, could not, risk giving the slow, dull idiot knowledge that could bring a mob shrieking and tearing at him out of the night sometime. Bo Jim could do that to him. To both of them. With all the best intentions in the world Bo Jim might someday open his mouth and tell someone about the woman. It could happen anytime.

Waring was small, almost puny — and stubborn and trying to protect his woman. The man might very well roll belly up and die on them before they could get the truth out of him. He might do it deliberate, hoping the woman might somehow have the gold after Jimbo and Bo Jim were gone. Or just for spite.

Jimbo was not good at something like this. He did not like to try to calculate and reason and decide on things. It was not his way. He preferred to find some tempting little score, hit it quickly and get away to enjoy whatever they took. He was used to that. He liked it, found it comfortable. This was something else entirely. Yet — he could not know, but he could feel it — this just might be his one chance to make a big score, a really big one. There could be a thousand dollars or more in Waring's poke.

People talked, he knew, about famous robbers and the huge sums they stole. Jimbo doubted that even the fabled bank and train robbers got away with half — a quarter — of what people claimed. Once a strongbox was gone the freight people could claim it had held any amount. Probably the James boys and those others had done the freight carriers a favor by robbing them. It was the insurance companies that got robbed in the end.

Jimbo knew for sure that he had made no big scores like that. The most he had ever seen in his life was a little more than eight hundred dollars, and he had had to split that with two other men. Why, once he and Bo Jim had tried to go big time. They held up a stage and got away with the cashbox. A newspaper story the next week said they got more than $2,000 in gold coin and currency. The box had held exactly $263. He remembered the amount quite well. And it *had* been a good score compared with most. Jimbo sighed. He wished he knew if he should start in on the man or on the woman. He was afraid of the possibility of failure with the one or a mob with the other. It was hard to decide which he should risk.

CHAPTER 26

With both coat pockets stuffed full of ragged chunks of horsemeat, Veach trudged toward the looming far wall of the narrow gorge. He had had difficulty hacking the frozen meat from the carcass, but had persisted at the unpleasant chore. Now he wanted to find a way to get warm — and to hide.

At the moment warmth was far more enticing. Either the cold was getting worse or he was feeling it more than before. He did not know which, but he knew he was miserably uncomfortable. His ears and nose were painful. His hands and feet were beyond pain. Fear of frostbite made him wish for the pain again. He would far rather hurt than lose fingers or toes.

Behind him he left a trampled path in the snow that would be impossible for a pursuer to mistake. Unless he wanted to return to the cabin, though, or to further backtrail the dead deputy, he had no choice but to cross virgin snow.

He stopped and snapped his fingers, but managed only a dull thud thanks to the padding of his gloves. He smiled to himself and turned back toward the path already broken by the deputy.

Veach had intended to work his way back downstream toward the beaten snow area where the horses and mules were foraging and perhaps find a way to lose his tracks amid theirs, if only temporarily. If he tried to backtrail the dead man the passage of a second person would be obvious.

Yet there might be a chance — a double chance — for survival in that direction, he realized. One would be if he found the bodies of the other members of the posse that had been following Fyle and Hatch. He had no way of knowing how far the deputy had come on his own, but if Veach reached one of the others he should surely find a gun there — a means to defend himself, perhaps even to attack the cabin, where he could be sure of finding food and warmth.

The other possibility was that he might find John Waring's diggings. Wherever Waring's mine was — he had come from the upstream direction when he returned to the cabin the first night Veach was there —

it was definitely a hard-rock dig. That had been quartz they had crushed that night, not drift or stream-bed material.

A shaft, even a shallow one, would mean shelter and probably a supply of wood. Even if Waring had not had need of firewood for his own comfort there, a shaft almost certainly would be shored up — with burnable wood. The thought of them was enough to add life to Veach's tiring legs. He would be happy to find either a gun or the mine. If he was really lucky he might find both. The increased pace made him feel almost warm.

Jimbo Fyle glowered at the pair on the bunk. This whole problem was their fault. A string of what-ifs tumbled through his thoughts. One thing he had decided for sure. He was not going to lose this chance to make a big score. John Waring was a smart man, maybe even a gentleman. Whatever he had out here had to be enough to set Jimbo up for a long time, enough to make him feel really *good.* It could be the start of bigger things in the future. Once a man got a taste of success it could be what he needed to spur himself on to more and to better things. And luck seemed to come in strings of good breaks. The snow had been one, stripping that posse off their backs and leaving them a clear path into Wyoming. John Waring and his cache was another. It was impossible to know what the next might be. Jimbo decided he would be ready for it, whatever it was, whenever it came. With his luck running strong he could set aside his worries, just make sure there was no one who could tell what happened here. Maybe . . . the thought struck him hard and he wondered why he had not thought of it before . . . maybe not even Bo Jim.

That would have been his biggest worry, of course. The lummox got so proud of Jimbo sometimes that he just had to brag on his friend's accomplishments. If he got so happy with Waring's poke that he mentioned the woman it could all come back on them. But there was no danger of Bo Jim saying anything if he stayed here with the Warings and with that fellow who had ducked out.

Jimbo felt mildly saddened by his realization. He and Bo Jim had been together quite a while now. Bo Jim had been useful — loyal and totally dependable within his limits. Still, Jimbo admitted, the man was strictly small time. He had no imagination, did not seem to care about anything beyond having something to eat, occasionally a blowout with liquor and a woman. He never seemed to miss what he did not have. Jimbo was not like that at all. He had his dreams of a good life backed by plenty of money, polished boots, fancy women and beds with sheets on them. With his luck running strong he could have that and more. Bo Jim could be a threat to that success. Jimbo could not allow that.

"I s'pose you oughta turn over your poke now," he said.

"What?" Waring's head snapped up in response and his eyes found Jimbo. He looked disoriented, as if his thoughts had been ranging deep and far, but not on the happenings in his own cabin. Jimbo had seen such before, puny little people without real strength, without Jimbo's strength, who refused to really believe what was happening to them. Waring sat up on the edge of the bunk and faced Jimbo. "I didn't realize you were talking to me, Fyle. What was it you wanted?"

"Johnny boy, you know what Jimbo an' Bo Jim want here. Whyn't you just save us all a bunch of bother an' hand it over. We're gonna have it. You know that. It'll just make things easier on ever'body if you was, uh, prudent about it, Johnny, an' give right in."

Jimbo smiled pleasantly. His attitude seemed one of benign helpfulness.

"Just like that?"

Jimbo's smile became broader. "Sure. Then we don't hafta hurt nobody. We get what we want. You stay safe an' happy. Everybody comes out ahead, don't you see?" His smile was warmly encouraging. Jimbo knew that the force of his own certainty, his own conviction that Jimbo Fyle was on a run of luck and would not, could not be successfully opposed, would be almost overwhelming. In rejecting what Jimbo expected, Waring could feel no more forceful than a wood shaving dropped into a mountain stream.

"I have no choice, Fyle," Waring explained slowly, as if explaining to himself as well. "You couldn't leave here now if you wanted to. We couldn't all stay here together afterward. It wouldn't be possible, no matter what promises you might make."

"Ah, Johnny. I wouldn't lie to you, boy. Jimbo don't do that, you see. I tell you what. Fair is fair, right? You do something for Jimbo, Jimbo does somethin' for you. You hand over your poke to Jimbo. Jimbo an' Bo Jim let you an' the little lady walk away from here. How 'bout that, Johnny?"

Jimbo could see in the man's eyes that

Waring was almost tempted to accept. Had it not been for his wife he might have. Instead he shook his head firmly. "Without a chinook wind, that would be certain death, and we both know it. Surely you can't expect me to take Ann out there."

Jimbo grinned. "Don't know why not, Johnny. Least you'd have a chance that way. Otherwise you couldn't hardly say that you do."

"I disagree. Of course you have the power to harm us, either or both of us, but that way you gain nothing except the likelihood of hanging. You wouldn't even get to see the little bit I have tucked away. I'd say we are still in your Mexican standoff, Fyle."

Jimbo shook his head sadly. "Sure do hate t' do this, Johnny." He stood and picked up the table, setting it easily aside out of his way. One long stride forward left him looming over Ann Waring. She seemed to sense his presence there. She opened her eyes and looked uncomprehendingly up toward him.

John Waring desperately launched a head butt toward the man's groin, flinging himself bodily at Fyle with all of his weight.

Fyle's clubbed left hand swept down, smashing into the side of Waring's head and flinging him aside as easily as another man might have brushed away an annoying child.

Waring hit the floor face down with no time to break the fall with his hands. His nose and mouth landed on a protruding rock, clacking his teeth together and sending a flow of hot, coppery blood into his mouth. The thick fluid was gritty with pieces of chipped and broken teeth. He rolled over and blinked, trying to clear away a misty haze that was distorting his vision. The inside of his skull seemed to be filled with a roaring noise like continuous thunder. He wanted to get up and throw himself again at Fyle. He tried to do so, persisting even though it seemed to be taking him a long while to rise. He was unaware that his body was no longer responding to his commands. He lay quite still from the shoulders downward. He tried to come to his feet and managed to move only his head. Far above him and coming nearer he could see the massive bulk of Bo Jim Hatch stirring, beginning to move with all the wild, fierce power of a grizzly. Waring groaned through crushed lips.

Jimbo laughed down at the battered man at his feet. He took the woman by her wrist and hauled her upright, holding her against him. "Time t' speak up, Johnny, or I start in on th' little lady here."

He took her roughly by the nape of her

neck and shoved down and forward until she was peering down over her husband's bloody features. "She ain't likely t' be pretty when I get done, Johnny. You gotta speak up, boy."

Waring worked his lips. He tried to speak — he wanted to tell Fyle — but no sound emerged.

Fyle grinned. "If this hasta be done," he said, "it might's well be fun." He reached forward with his free hand. Powerful fingers grasped the woman, squeezing cruelly into her flesh. Her face went white with pain.

Jimbo grunted and doubled over. More in puzzlement than in pain he looked up. Bo Jim had hit him, he finally realized. Too late to duck he saw Bo Jim's fist slam forward like a sledge-hammer to pulp his nose.

Jimbo felt a surge of strength caused not by anger but by joy. He loved physical combat. He enjoyed any brawl. And Bo Jim had given him a fine excuse to leave the slow and stupid man here — dead — when Jimbo left with Waring's gold. As soon as he got his breath Jimbo would naturally beat hell out of ol' Bo Jim. He'd done it before, hadn't he? It was Bo Jim's hard luck to be trying him again. And it was his own fault now.

Bo Jim fought without emotion. He was

301

not angry with Jimbo. He hoped Jimbo would not be angry with him later. But you just did not treat a lady like that. And Ann Waring *was* Bo Jim's own lady. Jimbo must have forgotten that. He must have forgotten that you do not treat a lady like you would handle some common woman.

Had he thought about it Bo Jim would have admitted that he was not sure how a lady *was* treated. He was sure, in some vague and undefined way, that a real lady was not the object of fleshly lusts. And he knew that Jimbo should not have touched this lady, Bo Jim's lady, in such a manner.

Bo Jim knew also that if he gave Jimbo time to set himself for the fight, Bo Jim was in trouble. Jimbo needed time to think about this quietly so he would understand. Bo Jim set his feet solidly and thudded blow after blow into Jimbo's unprotected windbasket.

Each of Bo Jim's crushing punches landed with much of the force of a mule's kick. One upon another they broke and tore the fiber of hard muscle, cracked and soon splintered tough bone, finally shocked and ruptured the tough valves of Jimbo Fyle's heart. Jimbo died on his feet. Neither he nor Bo Jim knew it at the time.

Fyle collapsed, and Bo Jim nodded solemnly with patient satisfaction. Jimbo could take time to think about it now. Bo Jim stepped back, ignoring both men on the floor at his feet. He turned and smiled at the lady.

CHAPTER 27

Ann Waring felt as if her thoughts had been swimming in a dark pool and she was just now reaching solid ground. She was aware of everything that had happened, but shock had held her detached, at arm's length, so that she had known but had not truly felt involved in what went on around her.

She looked down at her husband and felt a soft, warm flood of emotion such as she had never known before. John was bloodied, hurt and helpless. He had need of her now. He needed help. *Her* help. She had never before felt a sense of being truly necessary, not in this or any other matter.

She looked up and found Bo Jim watching her, his eyes patient, his expression impassive. She found her voice and breathed out a quick "thank you" that she reinforced with a brief squeeze of his arm. Outwardly Bo Jim did not respond, but she felt that she had pleased him. She dropped to her knees beside her husband.

Jimbo Fyle was lying across Waring's legs and lower torso, pinning the smaller man to the earth floor and making his breathing difficult. The woman saw at once that Fyle was dead.

"Move him for me please, Mr. Hatch," she ordered with an impatient gesture toward Fyle.

"Yes, ma'am. I'll lay him over here."

Bo Jim lifted Jimbo in his arms. Fyle's weight was a struggle even for him to manage. Bo Jim picked him up and moved him carefully to the front of the cabin, laying him down gently with Jimbo's head pillowed on Bo Jim's folded coat beside the door. He remembered to put Jimbo's revolver into his own waistband to keep Waring from getting to it later. Jimbo would be angry if he did not do that, he knew.

"Now move my husband onto the bunk, please."

"Yes, ma'am."

Bo Jim moved to obey. He placed Waring on the bunk where the deputy had lain and straightened the unconscious man's legs.

"Please build up the fire, Bo Jim, and I suspect we shall need more water. I want to heat what we have left in the bucket there."

Bo Jim nodded his acceptance of her

authority and did as she asked. He refueled the firebox and put water on to heat before he took the bucket and started toward the creek.

Bo Jim did not realize that Jimbo was dead, and he did not want to disturb his friend and perhaps further anger him. He left his coat cushioning Jimbo's head and went out into the cold in his shirt sleeves.

Ann Waring had a wet cloth and was starting to wash the blood from her husband's face when Bo Jim left. She watched the door close and heard Bo Jim test the latch from outside. Her eyes swept toward her trunks piled in the front corner of the cabin and toward the thing that was wedged between the trunks and the wall there.

John's rifle was there. There were cartridges for it in a box on one of the shelves. She had never fired that or any other weapon before, but she believed she could load it and could discharge it if she had to. She could do whatever was required of her, she was sure.

She decided to leave the rifle alone. Bo Jim could help her, already had saved her from whatever horrors Jimbo Fyle had intended. She felt sure that she was in no danger from Bo Jim now that Fyle was dead. She went back to bathing her husband's face.

The day passed slowly. Waring drifted in and out of sleep, but his color was good and when he was awake he was weak but coherent. In the afternoon she had Bo Jim lift his shoulders from the bed while she bound John's ribs with strips of torn cloth.

She cooked a large dinner and herself ate hugely of the fried steaks without once giving thought to where the meat had come from. She made a thin broth for her husband and spooned it into him while Bo Jim supported his head.

Bo Jim's eyes rarely left her. He openly watched every move she made, sat in contented silence staring at her when she was in repose. Once that would have bothered, even frightened her. At another time, had her mood and sense of protected security been right, Bo Jim's constant attention might have amused her. Now she simply was aware of it, accepted it as a fact and gave no further thought to it.

That evening, with Waring asleep and a heavy meal resting warmly in their stomachs, Bo Jim broke the silence to say, "It's good to have a lady. Me, I sure never thought to have one. I'm awful glad you took a liking to me." Anxiously he added, "You do like me, don't you? You said you did. I remember that real good."

A day, a month, a year before such a question would have petrified her. Now it did not. She laid her fork onto her plate and met Bo Jim's eyes. "Of course I like you, Bo Jim. And I am very flattered that you approve of me."

Bo Jim nodded seriously. "There's something I don't understand, though."

"You may ask if you wish."

"It's about your man. At night, I mean. What does a real lady do with her man?"

The question surprised her, but failed now to shock her. Playing for time she asked, "With John, you mean?"

"No. Me. I'm your man now, ain't I?"

A wave of coldness swept through her as completely as if she had been instantly transported beyond the cabin walls, but it did not show in her expression. She remained calm. "Ladies do nothing that is not proper," she said primly.

"No, ma'am. I know that."

"Fine."

"I mean, can I at least sleep *beside* you?" Bo Jim persisted.

Her thoughts flew. She glanced over at her husband. He was sleeping soundly. She did not want to disturb him. She especially did not want to give Hatch cause to further harm him. She was not worried, though. She would not allow things to get out of hand. John would be allowed to recover. "Beside me, yes. On the floor. But you may not paw me or touch me in any way," she said sternly.

Bo Jim nodded. He had expected no more. He moved eagerly to clean up the dishes, refill the woodbox and prepare a nest of blankets. He used both Veach's and Fyle's bedrolls for softness over the floor and his own for a top cover. His expression showed none of it, but he was atremble with excitement when she lay on the pallet he had prepared and allowed him to blow out the lamp.

Bo Jim was awake early. He lay for a time listening to the sound of the lady's breathing, so soft near his ear. Later, to escape the unwanted lustful urges that kept growing within him in spite of himself, he slipped silently off the shared bed and padded to the stove. He wanted the cabin warm when she wakened.

In the light from the open firebox door he checked the room. Jimbo was still sleeping, he saw. But on the bunk John Waring's eyes were open.

Bo Jim had no feelings toward Waring, neither good nor bad. He did not see the man as a factor in anything he wanted beyond the gold, and that Jimbo would take from Waring later. That sort of thing was up to Jimbo, anyway. He always took care of such. Bo Jim finished filling the firebox and eased the door closed quietly so he would not disturb the lady.

Waring had seen Hatch leave the bed with his wife sleeping, perhaps even unconscious, beside him. Waring tried to get up, to get to the rifle. He did not have the strength to lift himself from the bunk. In a low voice John Waring began to call curses down upon Bo Jim Hatch.

Hatch stepped carefully over the lady and went to stand over Waring. He listened to the man's anguished cursing and knew that he would have to kill Waring to defend his possession of the lady who had belonged to this man. Waring said over and over that he would kill Bo Jim. Bo Jim accepted the statements as fact. He did not resent or fear it. As soon as Jimbo woke up he would help his friend get Waring's gold. Then it would be all right to kill him. He cuffed the man once to shut him up.

The woman wakened and Bo Jim turned his attention to her, ignoring John Waring helpless on the bunk behind him.

Ann Waring sat and smoothed her dress.

She made sure her buttons were fastened and used her fingers to brush her tumbling hair back behind her ears. Later, she decided, she could take the time to do her hair properly. She glanced back toward John. He seemed to be still asleep, so she kept her voice low.

"Will cornmeal mush be all right for your breakfast, Bo Jim? John should be able to eat some of that when he wakens."

"Yes, ma'am," Bo Jim said. "An' make enough for Jimbo too. He's slept an awful long time. He'll be hungry when he gets up."

The woman was taken aback by the macabre thought of Bo Jim waiting for a dead man to wake up, a man he had killed himself. She did not know what to say, how to tell him.

Bo Jim was happier than at any time he could remember. He had a real lady and had just spent the night beside her. He felt light and free and cheerful. Conversationally he told the lady, "When Jimbo gets up he'll wanta get that gold from that fella."

"That fellow?"

"Him." Bo Jim hooked a thumb toward Waring.

"From my . . . ?" She caught herself in time to avoid saying "husband." She did not know how Bo Jim would react to hearing her name the relationship. She was afraid again — terribly afraid. She swallowed hard and said, "From John, you mean."

"Yeah. Him. Jimbo wants to talk to him. Then I'll have to kill him, I s'pose."

Her face blanched, but somehow she managed to keep herself under control. "I don't think you should do that," she said weakly.

"Got to," Bo Jim explained reasonably. "He said he'd kill me." He shrugged. It was obvious to him that he had no other choice. It was the only thing that made sense. There would have been no point in discussing it further. "If you're gonna make mush you need more water." He picked up the water bucket and went to the door, taking care to avoid Jimbo. He did not mind going out without his coat again. He did not want to disturb his friend.

Ann Waring watched with horror as the door shut behind him. She heard him fumbling at the latch to see that it was secure.

She felt the panic rise darkly within her. She tried to fight it back. John's eyes were open. He tried to get up, but could not. She wanted to vomit, but she knew that if she once started she would still be heaving when

312

Hatch returned. And when he returned and realized that Jimbo was dead he would kill John.

"The gun," Waring hissed. "Get my rifle."

Weak-kneed and feeling faint, she scrambled up from the pallet and stumbled toward the corner. She clawed aside the topmost trunk and grabbed for the cold, alien metal of the rifle barrel. Hatch must be halfway to the creek, she thought wildly.

"It isn't loaded."

"Where . . . ?"

"On the back wall shelf."

She whirled and banged the stock of the rifle viciously across her shin. She ignored the pain and ran across the cabin. The shelf was cluttered with boxes of matches, a stack of candles, a box holding a stereopticon and an assortment of photographed views that John had given her. She swept them aside. Her fingers closed on the heavy, pasteboard box of cartridges. She spilled them onto the table. The bucket might be full by now.

She put the rifle onto the table and snatched up a shell. She knew it went into the back end of the rifle, but she saw no opening there.

"You have to open the chamber," Waring said calmly. "Use the lever to open the chamber."

313

She let the cartridge fall from her fingers and turned the heavy rifle upside down on the tabletop. She grabbed the lever and pulled. It seemed frozen in place. It would not move.

"There is a release catch," Waring prompted gently. "At the back end of the lever. Push the little button and pull it back."

Tears of frustration were making it difficult for her to see. She wiped her sleeve across her eyes and did as she was instructed. She broke a nail on the catch, but slid it free.

"Now the lever. Pull up to open it."

She nodded. Hatch should be halfway back to the cabin. The lever moved easily at her touch.

"Turn it over."

"What?"

"The rifle. Turn it over. Put the cartridge into the chamber there. You'll see it."

She dropped the rifle and almost screamed. She rolled it over. It was as John had said. The chamber was there, open, ready to receive one of the fat, brass-and-lead cartridges. Her fingers flew to the table and fumbled for a cartridge. She found one. Hatch could be at the door now.

Involuntarily she glanced up toward the

door. A moment more was all she needed. Her heart felt as if it had stopped. She cried out. The door latch was lifting.

CHAPTER 28

Bo Jim felt good. Strong and vigorous and . . . good. Nothing could have been better than this. He had the lady all for his own and when Jimbo woke up they would have the gold. That would please Jimbo. He would not stay mad at Bo Jim for hitting him then.

Bo Jim picked up the bucket and set it outside. Before he pulled the door closed he got a last glimpse of the lady. Not only was she a real lady, she was beautiful too. He had wanted desperately to touch her hair the night before.

He was sure she would let him do that soon. It was proper to do that, he knew. The other man, the one that had been her husband, had brushed her hair the other day. He did it while they were all watching, too, so it had to be a proper thing that one could do with ladies. Bo Jim could almost feel the way her hair would be under his fingers, softer and smoother than anything he had ever felt before, golden in the lamp-light. That was finer gold than the kind Jimbo wanted. And Bo Jim was going to have both. Golden lady. Golden money. He wondered if her hair would be warm to the touch, or cool.

Bo Jim pulled the door closed behind him, regretting the necessity to lose sight of her while he fetched the water. But he could not expect a lady to go out with him in the cold to draw water. That would not be proper. And the trip would take only a mo-ment. Perhaps when he got back Jimbo would be awake, and they could have break-fast together. He would have the lady fry steaks again. Jimbo would be awfully hungry after sleeping through both dinner and sup-per yesterday. He would want red meat and lots of it. There was plenty available. When what they had ran out Bo Jim could go get more. He would want his coat when he did that, though.

Bo Jim flexed his shoulder muscles be-neath the thin covering of his shirt. Right now, while he was still warm from being in the cabin, the cold felt more invigorating than annoying. He liked it.

Slowly and very, very thoroughly he latched the cabin door and tested to make sure the latch had securely closed. Bo Jim had long since forgotten the night long years before when a seven-year-old had forgotten to relatch a shoat pen, allowing two of the pigs to escape while the others ruined most of a stand of scratch corn, nor did he remember the beating his father had given him with a length of broken fence paling. But always he remembered to test the latch when he closed a door or a gate.

He picked up the bucket and smiled to himself. He would be back with the lady soon. He turned.

Bo Jim barely had time to register awareness of what was before him. A man, bulky in a heavy coat, burlap sacking tied around his feet and legs and draped over his head and ears for added protection from the cold. The man was swinging something at him, bright steel flashing in a silver arc through the early morning sunlight. Bo Jim did not have time to duck.

The heavy miner's pick sank into the hollow of the big man's throat with a loud but curiously dull thwock.

Bo Jim dropped in a straight fall. His knees sank into the frozen snow and he toppled forward, his head and upper body suspended above the ground surface against the blunt, mattock end of the pick. Bright red began to stain the snow, quickly darkening and freezing.

Veach stepped back away from the body. He looked at it and began to gag at the sight of what he had done. If he had not been afraid that Jimbo Fyle might at any moment put his head out of the door, Veach very likely would have given in to the impulse and allowed himself to disgorge the half raw horsemeat he had had for breakfast before he left Waring's mine.

He dropped to his knees beside Hatch's body. His breathing was labored, although he had had ample time to rest after his trek, and he was trembling all over. The fear of Jimbo Fyle made him find the strength to shuffle forward on his knees to pull Hatch's revolver from its holster.

With the gun in his hand he felt somewhat better. He rocked back on his heels, eyes fixed on the closed door, ears tuned to catch the first hint of rattle from a rising latch. He began to get his breathing under control.

He climbed to his feet, feeling weary and far from ready for a fight, but he had the revolver as a comforting presence in his grip and he was too cold to wait much longer. One way or another he wanted to get it over with. He transferred the gun to his left hand and used his teeth to strip the glove from

319

his right so he would have a better hold on the heavy revolver.

With mingled fear and determination he stepped forward, steeled himself and lifted the latch. The door swung open. He was ready to fire.

From the dimly lighted interior he heard John Waring's voice. "It's all right, dear. It's all right now."

On the back of his neck Veach felt the first stirrings of a rising breeze. A warm breeze. He stepped inside and closed the door.

ABOUT THE AUTHOR

Frank Roderus wrote his first story at the age of five. A newspaper reporter for nine years, he now lives in Colorado Springs, where he raises American Quarter Horses and pursues his favorite hobby, researching the history of the American West.